Van Nair

THE SNAKE AROUND THE PIPER'S ROD

AUSTIN MACAULEY PUBLISHERS®

LONDON · CAMBRIDGE · NEW YORK · SHARJAH

ISBN – 9789948774570 – (Paperback)
ISBN – 9789948774587 – (E-Book)

Application Number: MC-10-01-0603375
Age Classification: 17+

The age group that matches the content of the books has been classified according to the age classification system issued by the UAE Media Council.

Printer Name: iPrint Global Ltd
Printer Address: Witchford, England

First Published 2024
AUSTIN MACAULEY PUBLISHERS FZE
Sharjah Publishing City
P.O Box [519201]
Sharjah, UAE
www.austinmacauley.ae
+971 655 95 202

1

HOWL. A wolf called out. The trees whistled their solemn song as they waited for anyone, anyone at all, to pass by their morbid frames. Their hands lacked any leaves, and they stood like bare sentinels, guarding the town. A bright full moon shone in the sky, bone-white, casting a pale light onto the pavement. The air felt thick, heavy, and laden. Oh, what was this night?

The grass on the field was blown away by the fury of the wind, but, in the middle of the lawn, a white house stood courageous. It was quite small, but it looked lively; a window by the right glowed with a yellow shade, and figures moved about inside. Smoke rose from the chimneys, battling away the mist in the air, closely followed by the scent of sweet, freshly baked cinnamons, a smell that seemed welcoming.

From inside the house came the sounds of plates clattering and people speaking over one another as they shared a dish or two. Occasionally, this was accompanied by jocund shouts of children. Ah, at least this house, be it the only one or not, was happy.

But somewhere among all this happy noise came a *plok*, and then another.

It was the footsteps of a brave soul, one that dared to face this dreadful night.

Slowly, the footsteps got louder and louder, until finally, a figure could be seen at the end of the road. Actually, two figures. The first one was tall, just the right build, with a shoulder that you wouldn't call too wide or too crushed. Following him was a smaller shadow, with a small head, and thin arms.

The two figures made their way to the garden gate, still content with their slow strides. The pale light of a streetlamp fell onto their faces now. The taller man had a curved chin and a medium-sized nose. Nothing special, until you realized that his face was gray. The kind of gray that makes you want to turn away. And then, there was the nail, a long metal piece inserted into his head. On one side of his skull, you could see the head of the nail, and on the other side, you could see its sharp end. One could only shudder. He wore a brown vest and torn brown jeans. Nothing else. His chest, exposed, was gray as well.

You could see his companion clearly too. He was a dwarf compared to the man, but they looked starkly similar. There was just one big difference: the dwarf looked… looked… darker. He wore a black robe with a red collar, and his skin was ghostly. The dwarf looked at the man with the screw in the head and grinned. This only made things scarier because you could see the companion's teeth, curved and sharp. It could be compared with a tiger's claw, but that would do it no justice. It looked menacing as it glistened in the moonlight.

The two monsters made their way up the drive, walking casually up to the front porch. As they stepped in, the floorboards creaked. The gray man winced but kept going. He reached out to the doorbell, but before giving it a press, he turned to his little friend. The man nodded, just a bit, but the friend understood and nodded back. *DING DONG.*

As soon as the doorbell was pushed, the two monsters jumped to either side of the doorframe, vanishing into the darkness that enveloped the house. One second, two seconds. They waited patiently. The gray man did not make a sound, but the companion giggled with childish excitement.

The gray man shushed at this, and everything became lifeless again. For some seconds, nothing could be heard. Then, from the silence, the door was bolted open, and it swung inside.

The monsters shuffled, and they stopped breathing. A bright yellow light filled the porch, and a plump silhouette of a woman stood between the doorframes. The monsters looked poised. Someone was going to be dinner… and soon.

2

The woman stepped out. She squinted her eyes, and her eyebrows were raised up. She was about to peer to either side of the doorframe.

"Trick or Treat!" screamed the monsters together, jumping out from their hiding places. The pumpkin basket in their hands jingled with the promising sound of sweets. Their smiles were stretched across their faces, and their eyes were shining.

The woman put a hand on her chest and gave a laugh of relief.

"Oh, you boys gave me a scare!" the woman exclaimed, scanning the two 'monsters' from head to toe. She looked at the little boy in the black cape, bent down, and said, "You look absolutely adorable, Timmy!" She reached out and grabbed Timmy by the cheeks. Timmy winced but giggled. His cheeks went red, matching his cape collar.

Then she looked at the man. "Wow, Moose. You look… You look terrifying!" The woman acted like she was going to faint. Now, it was Moose's turn to smile. He looked at himself. He did put in a lot of effort to make this costume.

"Thank you, Sally!" Moose said and paused. He opened his mouth to say something but closed it again.

Sally looked around the deserted streets. "What a silent Halloween! Where is everybody?" Moose looked around too. Not even a single person was out, and there were no lights in most of the houses. Sally looked back at the two. "You are the only ones who told me 'trick and treat' today." She shrugged, not knowing what more to say.

"Auntie Sally, where are the sweets?" Timmy asked. He jingled his basket in front of Sally's eyes.

"I almost forgot!" Sally turned back and grabbed a box of lollipops. She poured it into the hungry mouth of Timmy's basket.

Moose slumped his shoulders. "Where's mine, Sally? I want some, too."

Sally looked at Moose, smiling. She shook her head. Wasn't Moose too old to go trick-or-treating anyway? She emptied the rest of the lollipop box into Moose's outstretched hand. "Ah, Moose. You are always the same, aren't you?" Sally looked at Timmy. "Your father's a bit childish, isn't he, Timmy?"

Timmy looked at his father, then burst out laughing. Moose turned the color of ripe tomatoes. He turned around to ruffle Timmy's hair, and Timmy, seeing what his father was going to do, ran out onto the front porch, laughing.

"You can't catch me, Daddy!"

Moose looked back at Sally, sighing. A bit excitedly, she said, "How was my conversation this time, Moose?" Sally was twiddling with her fingers now. She seemed to be expecting a positive answer.

"It was fantastic, Sally. It seemed really realistic," Moose assured with a smile.

"Really? I am so glad! I have been trying to experiment with all the different lessons we learned back in the speaking club. You know how I am, right, Moose? Always getting flustered." Sally was speaking with the exuberance of a kid now. "I don't know, Moose. I didn't stutter this time, right?"

Moose gave a thumbs-up. "It was great. Stop worrying, Sally. You're amazing at speaking."

Sally beamed.

"Daddy, why are you taking so long? We need to go to one more house. You promised," Timmy whined from the garden gate. Moose turned around and looked at Timmy. Then, he looked at Sally with a sad smile, as if he wanted to say sorry.

Sally understood. "No problem, Moose. You better hurry. It is getting quite late. You don't want Timmy to be sad, do you?"

Moose glanced at his watch—half past nine. "I am sorry, Sally. Anyway, we will meet each other at our next club meeting, right? Saturday, isn't it?"

"Yes, Saturday. I can't wait!"

And with that, Moose joined Timmy near the garden gate, and the duo waved at Sally. Then, they left on their way and continued up the abandoned street.

On their way up, they passed many houses. Many of them were boring, and old, and normal. But… amongst all these houses was one that looked sadder than the rest. One of its windows was cracked, and the garden stood all dried up. A few broken pieces of china, probably from a garden gnome, lay here and there. Moose couldn't hold back a shudder. It was the house of the stranger. Yes, that was what the owner of the house was known as—just 'the stranger.' He never came out of his house, and Moose had only seen him once. But even in that one opportunity he got, he didn't catch his face. Most people smelled a rat when they talked about the stranger. Moose didn't really know what to think of him. He was just a bit… creepy.

Standing in front of the door was a boy. He was covered from head to toe in toilet paper.

A typical mummy costume.

As Moose and Timmy passed by, the boy, hearing their footsteps, peeked back and waved. Moose knew him. A really nice kid, too. He was from the orphanage; his parents had abandoned him when he was just three months old. It was terribly unfortunate. He had to live in the orphanage ever since.

Moose and Timmy waved back. The boy smiled pleasantly and turned back to face the door.

Moose and Timmy kept walking. Through the fog, they were able to see nothing; the fog was mugging their eyesight. Moose didn't need to see. He already knew what was coming up ahead. Through the fog came the faint outline of a basket hanging on a pole. This was the only major landmark on Lollipop Avenue, and everyone knew it.

Moose took a handful of lollipops and placed them in the basket. It was a sort of a tradition here; whoever passed by the basket could take or place a lollipop. Maybe that was why the town was called Lollipop Avenue, Moose thought, as he started licking a lollipop himself. Or maybe the name came from the lollipop factory nearby. Or, oh, maybe it was named by some children. There were quite a lot of kids here. Moose didn't know, and he didn't think he would know anytime soon.

After some time of walking, they passed by a signpost. Moose stopped, and looked up at it, reading the only sign on the board. It said *'Handsome Manor'* in faded lettering, and it was hard to see where it was pointing to with all the mist. Moose squinted in the direction of the signboard, as much as his eyes would let him, and he knew that the Manor was somewhere out there. Timmy was still walking, but he realized that Moose had stopped. He glanced with a frown at his father's face, which was contorted in thought. "Timmy, do you think we ought to give Handsome Manor a visit?"

Timmy looked into the distance too, and then he gulped. He kept staring into the mist for some time. Suddenly, he looked around him and, shuddering, he came closer to Moose. He looked Moose in the eye. He gave a half-nod, and then he started to nod a bit more confidently. He gulped again.

The house was officially christened as the Handsome Manor. But the people here liked to call it a bit differently.

The Haunted House.

3

Turning the corner, the duo made their way through the dense woods that surrounded the Haunted House. They had decided to go. On either side of the two monsters stood tall, wide trees and the path below their feet had only gravel. There was no proper road in this part of town.

Timmy kept pulling at Moose's sleeve, nagging him. "Daddy, could you tell me the story of the Haunted House? Please?"

"No, Timmy. I have already told you the story, like, a million times. Aren't you bored already?"

Timmy looked into Moose's face with his beady eyes. Moose looked back at Timmy's eyes for a split second too long, and realizing that he was falling into a trap, he looked away into the trees on the other side. But, he could still feel Timmy's look at the back of his head.

Moose sighed. Timmy smiled, happy that he had gotten Moose to finally agree. "Daddy, don't forget the torch."

Moose thought about the torch. "What torch? I don't have a torch. Sorry, Tim Tim. I think I forgot to bring it."

Timmy stopped in his tracks and looked his father in the eye. "Daddy, I know there's a torch in your jacket pocket."

Moose gave an even louder sigh. He reached into his jacket and took out the torch. Why did he have to bring a torch with him? Switching it on, he lighted up his face with it. It had outlined all of Moose's bland features, and it darkened the edges of his face. Something about the light made Moose look scarier than he was. Moose focused his eyes on Timmy's and gave a slick smile. It was the joker's smile.

Then, he started.

"There once was a baron who lived in Lollipop Avenue. A very famous one. Baron James VI. He was a fearful baron, one that scared even the bravest of men. He led his army into many battles and won a lot of money for our town. And with this money, he started to build a castle in these very woods. People loved Baron James VI. He was a hero.

"But nobody knew about the other side of the baron." Moose smiled. It wouldn't be too far off if you thought it was the smile of a lunatic. "Only his own soldiers knew about the Baron's true personality. When the baron would give an order, everyone had to follow it. If anyone didn't…" Moose threw back his head and cackled. The wolves called from the distance, joining Moose.

Moose put his arms in front of him and acted like he was going to strangle Timmy. "If anyone dared to misbehave, the baron would take them to a special room hidden below the castle. Then, all you could hear of the one who misbehaved would be their screams. Screams that tore through the night." Hoot. Hoot. The owls hooted.

"And don't even think about seeing that soldier ever again. If you are lucky, you could get his eyeball or his fingers, but nothing else. But the other soldiers couldn't do anything to the baron, for they had sworn an oath when they had joined the army; if the baron was killed, they would die as martyrs too."

"But, fed up of the baron's heinous acts, the soldiers—"

Moose rubbed his palms together with the slyness of a snake. "—Hatched a plan, an ingenious plan. They talked with discretion and whispered with excitement in the middle of the night. They were going to do it."

"It was a cold autumn day. The time had come for them to do the thing they had been planning for. As night crept in, thunderstorms and lightning filled the air." Crackle. Moose looked up at the dark clouds above. It was going to rain soon. "The leader of the soldiers walked up to the room of the baron, stepped in slowly, and"—Moose drew his hand across his neck—"slit his throat. That was the end of the baron, the great, bad baron."

"The soldiers, not forgetting their oaths, decided to do something you never thought they would do. They decided to die too. Each one of them slit their throats and sacrificed their lives, all one thousand of them. Not even a single one of them betrayed the oath."

"It is said that once every year, on Halloween, when there is a full moon," Moose looked up at the silver disk, fully complete in the sky, "the souls of the one thousand soldiers and the baron rise up from their graves as ghosts and roam the Haunted House. It is said that the soldiers' screams of torture can still be heard in the Manor's corridors. A high-pitched song of sadness, playing eternally…"

Whoosh. Whoosh. Timmy jumped and looked to the other side of the woods. The wind was playing its melancholy composition as it scraped past the trees. Timmy squinted. He thought he saw… some eyes through the trees. It was gone.

Timmy turned back, but he didn't see his father. He looked around him. *THUMP, THUMP, THUMP.* His heart was pumping fear now. His eyes bulged.

"Daddy. Daddy!" Timmy didn't know what to do. All he could do was look back the way they had come. "Daddy, Dad…" Timmy lost his hope. He looked at the dense packet of trees. Had someone taken his father away?

Suddenly, Timmy felt something at his shoulder and turned around with lightning speed. Seeing that there was someone, Timmy lost his balance and fell to the floor. He looked up.

The night was filled with… with laughter? Moose was laughing out of control now. He was bent and was holding his stomach, trying to stop. "Wow. You should have seen the look on your face, Tim Tim," Moose said, wiping away the tears that had formed out of humor.

Timmy got up and crossed his arms. He put on a sour face, and his eyebrows were pointing downwards. He stood looking away.

"Oh, Timmy. I was just joking with you."

Timmy didn't budge.

"Now, whose father's boy? Who can't be angry with their father?" Moose chimed, ruffling Timmy's hair. Timmy smiled just a bit but took on the serious face again. Moose knew it was working. He started tickling Timmy, and Timmy's upside-down mouth had all but risen again. Timmy smiled.

Setting out on their way again, the duo walked in silence. The only noise came from the ravens calling behind the trees and the crickets. A rustling in the bushes to the right caught their attention. The two looked, a bit scared. Moose twisted his face in confusion. He had only told the story to scare Timmy. Now, who was this? They held their breaths and Moose grabbed a stick from the floor, careful not to take his eyes off the bush.

A rabbit jumped out of the bushes, and the father and son exhaled. Phew. Timmy leaped closer and picked up the fluffy creature. "Aw. Doesn't this rabbit look cute, Daddy? Who's a cute boy? Who's adorable?" Timmy tickled the rabbit's nose. "Rabbits are the nicest animals in the world."

Moose looked at the rabbit's black eyes. The rabbit was staring at him. Its eyes seemed to be trapping him in their never-ending blackness. Moose was starting to sweat. He couldn't escape the rabbit's gaze. The rabbit's mouth went up to one end as if it was grinning. Laughing at him. Mocking him. He gulped. Rabbits looked beautiful on the outside, but he knew there was a lot of evil somewhere deep down. It was just a feeling of intuition, but it didn't go away. He shuddered.

Timmy put the rabbit onto the ground and the duo watched it leap to the other side of the path. As the rabbit made its way, a red liquid traced its path. It was like a crimson brushstroke on the floor. Moose looked more closely. The rabbit wasn't injured. Otherwise, there should have been blood on Timmy's shirt, too. Moose shook his head and looked again. He blinked a couple of times, losing faith in his own vision.

The rabbit stopped as it neared the bush, and Moose took the opportunity to scan it. It was holding something in its paw, and Moose tried to make out what it was. His mouth gaped open, bit by bit, as the cogs in his head started spinning. Was that… Moose didn't even want to believe it, but he thought it was… it was… meat. Rabbits don't eat meat. No, they don't.

Moose stood still as a rock for some time, contemplating this mystery. Timmy was getting impatient, and Moose decided to keep walking. The rabbit jumped into the bushes as quickly as it had come when it had seen their frames getting closer. Moose dragged his feet forward, but his mind was still thinking about the rabbit. Finally, he sighed. He was never going to understand this.

4

Moose had forgotten the rabbit a long time ago by the time they had reached a silver gate. It rose up quite some feet and was pointed at the top, somewhat like a pitch fork. A gold plaque shone brightly on one side of the gate. *HANDSOME MANOR,* it said. They had reached their destination. They had reached the Haunted House.

Moose tried to stand on tiptoes and look over the gate, but his neck was too short to pass the metal structure that tried to compete in height with him. He stepped closer and caught the gate with both hands as if it was a jail door. He shook the gate. "Hello? Is anyone there?"

"Stop it. Stop it, you!" growled a voice from the distance. Moose turned around and saw a round guard bobbing his way to him. The torch in the guard's hand bobbed up and down too, and the guard was scowling. Moose thought he might probably get hit on the head by the torch if he didn't stop shaking the gates, so he put his arms down as quickly as possible.

"What do you want?" the guard demanded, still scowling.

Moose stumbled but caught himself. He didn't expect the guard to be this rude. "Sir, it's… I am—"

"Why are you here? I don't care about who you are," the guard snapped.

Moose felt his throat becoming dry. "We just want to see Dr. Sam… for Halloween… that's all. We will be out soon… 10, no, five minutes." Perspiration filled Moose's forehead.

The guard looked at Moose and Timmy from top to bottom. He was scanning them as if they had come to beg. The guard's eyes arrived back at their faces, but he didn't stop squinting. He still didn't believe them. Then, he turned around and slugged his way to the room at the side of the gate. The police room.

Moose was left to wonder if he would come back again, or whether he had decided to leave them out there in the cold as some kind of medieval punishment. Moose crossed his arms and decided to wait. He could see the guard through the window. He was calling someone with his walkie-talkie. Moose decided to listen in.

"Boss, there are… waiting to see you… should I…" Moose could only hear some parts of the conversation. Nevertheless, he knew who was on the other end—Sam. Dr Sam Hampton, the owner of the Haunted House.

"OK, boss… Yes, boss… Sure, boss." The guard had put down the handset and was walking back towards them now. But in slow motion. The guard didn't utter a word and went straight to the gate. He unbolted it and pulled it open. He stood to the side, but even then, he did not speak. He just looked into the forest to the side of the gate. His face never smiled in between, not even once.

Moose looked at Timmy, and he gestured for Timmy to follow him. The two walked to the gate and stepped over the guard. As they were coming closer, the guard pulled his nose up, as if smelling something filthy. Moose decided to ignore the guard. He took his eyes off the guard's face and looked forward.

For one second, Moose's mouth gaped open, just like it always had whenever he had seen the Handsome Manor. His eyes couldn't get enough. Timmy's mouth was also wide open. There, laying out before them, was a tall building that rose to the sky. It stretched from one end of Moose's vision to the other and filled their view completely. It felt purely majestic, a castle from a fairytale. Well, a castle that looked like a lollipop. Yes, the whole frame was colored in bright red and yellow, and it didn't feel like something you would expect to see in a sleepy village like Lollipop Avenue. At the top, a single yellow light shined brightly, and it stood out, for it was the only one.

Sam had spent a lot of money refurbishing the entire mansion. Or rather, the entire castle. He had turned the large wooden gates acting as the entrance into small (and altogether less scary) doors. He had covered the stone walls etched with history in the modern day's finest invention: wallpaper. Why, he was also the person who decided to paint the house red and yellow so that it looked more appealing to children. Moose had never forgotten the gray and desolate look the house had held before Sam moved in. Moose felt a chill run down his spine as the image of the castle's former image took shape in his mind's eye. Enough. No need to think about sadness and gloom, he thought.

The path to the entrance was covered on both sides by pine trees, the finest ones. Pumpkins lined the walkway, each one of them mocking Moose and Timmy with their crooked smiles and lopsided eyes. Moose looked at the house silently and imagined the treasures that stood behind it. Sam had probably built a jacuzzi or a swimming pool behind, for all Moose knew. It wouldn't be much of a surprise if a golf court was there too.

Moose wasn't making fun of Sam. Sam was a nice person. He was always willing to help, and he would lend a hand faster than many others. But it was this quality itself that made Moose a bit… reluctant. Something about Sam made Moose a bit apprehensible. He didn't know… Maybe Moose was just being jealous. Or maybe not.

Moose looked at Timmy. Timmy was holding a rueful look. Moose knew why—he was sad that he couldn't scare his Uncle Sam. The duo pulled themselves up the stairs and rang the bell, shoulders hunched. This time, they didn't step to the sides of the door or hold their breaths. What was the point? Sam already knew they were coming. After some time, the door was opened, and a plump little man stepped out. He wore a green Christmas sweater, and round glasses were perched on his nose. Only weeds of hair stuck out from his shiny, bald head. He threw his arms wide and smiled at the two with a smile that would make the people in toothpaste advertisements cry with joy. Moose half-expected him to start saying, "ho, ho, ho."

Seeing their sad faces, Sam said, "Oh, you two, why do you look so sad? Come on, cheer up!"

Moose just sighed. "Well, we wanted to surprise you. But… anyway, trick-or-treat."

Sam looked at Timmy's face, which was pointed downwards, and tutted. His smile started to fade.

Suddenly, his eyes lit up again, and he showed a finger to the two, asking them to wait. He disappeared into the house.

Moose looked at Timmy, Timmy looked at Moose. Whatever had happened to Sam?

Sam arrived after a few seconds, holding something behind him. "Uncle Sam knows what will make you happy!" He revealed a box with a golden covering. It shone in the darkness like some kind of precious chest.

Sam tipped half of the contents of the box into Timmy's pumpkin basket. Timmy looked at Moose, and then he looked at the chocolates, and then at Moose again. Just like Timmy, Moose was dazzled, too. The chocolates were wrapped in dark violet paper, and there was a small silver gift ribbon tied at the top. It was obvious that it was premium chocolate. Ah, it wasn't so shocking considering the fact that it was Sam who bought it.

"Thanks, Uncle Sam!" Timmy caroled. Sam beamed.

"Sam, you better keep some for the other kids. You don't want to end up disappointing them, do you?" Moose advised.

"There's enough for everybody, Moose. Don't you worry. I just hope they come here, too!" Sam was gleaming now.

Moose looked at his watch. It was getting late. "OK, Sam. We better get going. Got to take supper."

"No problemo. I made some roasted chicken with avocado dressing. You are welcome to join me if you want." Sam looked at the two, his face illuminated with an electric smile.

"No. No thank you, Sam," Moose said, trying to suppress his stomach's wail.

The two were about to leave when Sam spoke again. "Well, do you need a ride home, fellas?"

Moose looked at Timmy's pleading eyes. Timmy was silently *begging* him to say 'yes'. Moose looked back at Sam with a blunt expression, and said, "No, Sam. We will be fine walking."

Moose turned around and walked halfway down the front path when he noticed that Timmy was not with him. He turned around again and spotted Timmy still standing on Sam's front porch. "Are you coming, Timmy?" he called out, extra loudly.

Timmy stood still for a moment, and then he ran back to Moose. "Daddy, Uncle Sam's the nicest man in the world. Why couldn't we go in his car?" he whispered.

Moose just looked straight and shrugged. Sam was shouting something from behind, and Moose looked back. Sam was waving, still with an electric smile. "See you at the office, Moose!"

Oh, Moose had forgotten to mention that. Sam was his colleague. Why, o, why did Sam have to be his colleague?

5

Moose stepped into the large, white room, quite similar to the ones docs use for examinations. Desks were arranged on both sides in cubicles that looked neat and tidy. The floor was covered in a black rug that absorbed the impact of any shoe that lay on it. A clean clock hung on one of the walls, and some blue cabinets with micropipettes accompanied the windows. An oak reception was placed at a corner, medical molecular models lining its surface. Chairs were neatly tucked beneath the tables, but they held a sad pose without anyone to sit on it. The only sound in the air was the low-key whistle of the AC. It was a typical medical laboratory and office, and some people would go so far as to say that it was the most typical medical office. A smile looped itself onto Moose's face, and he relaxed his shoulders. But to him, his office was special. He slowly made his way to his desk. As he passed the clock, he looked at its black dials. Moose's smile grew. He was 30 minutes early to the lab, a new record.

Moose sat down in front of his desk, kept his white lanyard (which was stickered with health badges of all shapes and sizes) on the table's side, and started his computer. He took out some papers from his bag and started writing away on his computer. He had to submit a drug sales report to Mr.

Riley, his boss. The deadline was only two weeks away. He was a bit late for this task, he thought sadly.

Moose didn't notice the time. All he was focused on was his task. Soon, all sorts of people in shirts of various colors walked into the office. Moose looked up whenever anyone entered and wished them wholeheartedly. Amongst the people who entered, one walked straight up to Moose and took a seat near him. He wore a rose-colored shirt, and he had sleek brown hair. He grabbed a sticky note with a red health-cross from the table and started playing with it. He took one paper out, then tried to make something. Not satisfied, he would crumple it and throw it onto the ground, and then take another sticky note. The ground was piled with red crosses within minutes. "Hello, George," Moose said, still not taking his eyes off the computer.

"Hey, Moose. How you doing?"

Moose just smiled and didn't look away from the computer screen. He knew George would understand him. After all, George had been with him for a long time now.

"You know, I always wonder why you take work so seriously. Why can't you just talk to me?" George asked, smiling.

"Well, I am talking to you, George."

George sighed. Moose smiled. "Well, I was quite surprised to see you sitting here. I thought you might have gone to the meeting already, you know, 15 minutes early, as usual." George laughed at his own joke.

Moose looked at George. "There's a brief today?"

George nodded. Moose looked at his watch. He still had five minutes. He immediately closed his laptop and stood up. He placed the laptop back into his bag.

"Oh, *come on*! You're going to the meeting, aren't you?" George asked. "I wish I hadn't told you about it."

Moose asked George if he was coming with him. George said, "Well, you go ahead. I am going to come 15 minutes *late*, as usual."

Moose left George to his red sticky notes and walked down the aisle to the meeting room. It was on the end of the office, right after the medical research department, which was the life blood of his company. His company was responsible for making medicines: drugs, pills, syrups, and the sort. Of course, Moose wasn't a medic, he was in sales. But there was one person who was in the medical research department, and when Moose thought about who it was, he didn't feel all that nice.

Sam.

There he was, waiting outside the department's main cabin, just back after his early morning consultations. You could see by the stethoscope dangling around his white coat collar. Moose tried to hide his face with the folder in his hand. But a simple folder couldn't stop Sam from sprinkling his goodness at Moose. Sam waved happily, and said, "Hi, Moose! Howdy?"

Moose lowered the file in defeat. He smiled a fake smile. He couldn't manage a better one. "Hello, Sam. I am fine. Thank you." Moose didn't stop at all, he kept continuing. Sam was one of the senior physician-scientists of the company, but he always acted modestly. Moose sighed. Too modestly.

Moose opened the door to the meeting room. The air was his only friend because there were no people in the room. Moose sat down at the first chair he could find and waited. He waited for some time, and, one by one, people started to enter the room. The empty chairs began to fill up. Moose got more people to say 'hi' to. Finally, a man dressed in a plain shirt and a wrinkled blazer came in. His tie was perfect, albeit bright, but his coat seemed to be a bit big for him. He had a wide build, and his face looked flat. His nose looked flat, his mouth looked flat, and his ears looked flat. But his eyes, his eyes looked sharp. It seemed to pierce through the person looking at it. As he came in, he smiled, and Moose couldn't help but smile too.

"Good mornin', everyone. How're my heroes today?" the man asked, smiling.

A chorus of answers floated in the air. Moose added a small, "I am fine, Mr Riley," in between all the noise.

Mr. Riley continued, his smile turning serious. "Well, today's the month-end. And that means only one thing. Award time."

The air got tense, and everyone shuffled in excitement. There was a low buzzing in the room now.

"So, ahem, ahem, we come to the prize ceremony. The employee-of-the-month, who will it be? Will it be you"—the boss was pointing at different people—"you, you, you, or you?" Each person who the boss looked at would freeze. There was a childish excitement on their faces, a curiosity to know if they really are the 'chosen one' (Mr Riley's words).

"The employee-of-the-month is… can I have a drum roll, please?" People started banging the tables or drumming on their laps. *BANG, BANG, BANG, BANG, BANG.*

"The award goes to," Mr Riley started again, "Goes to… Mr Moosehorn Roosevelt!"

What?

Moose's cheeks went the color of tomatoes, and the room felt like it was a furnace all of a sudden. Moose's muscles seemed to have turned to stone. At first, the claps went PAT, PAT, PAT, but as they turned into a roar, Moose's heart filled with a sort of pride. Someone pushed him from the crowd, and he was thrown off his seat. Moose's cheeks burned even more after that. He inched his way closer to Mr Riley, looking at both sides at the numerous faces who were smiling at him, clapping for him. "That's my Moose! Don't be shy," Mr Riley exclaimed. Mr Riley held Moose's shoulder and presented him with the certificate. It glowed so brightly that it seemed to be emitting light by itself. Moose held it with both hands, and it started shaking, just like his hand.

Moose smiled back at all the people standing in the crowd and vouching for him. "Go, go, Moose! Go, go, Moose!" chanted some of his extra extroverted colleagues. Moose couldn't help but smile.

He looked at all his workmates in turn, thinking about how kind they were to clap for someone like him. He saw George. George was clapping a bit slowly, and he kept looking around him. Oh, poor George. He didn't like loud noises, it must be hurting him. But the clapping just refused to stop. Ah, life is good indeed.

After Moose had got around a million 'congratulations, Moose' and a dozen pats on the back, it was time to leave the lab. Moose looked out of the window. Night had taken over the country, filling it with darkness and desperation. Moose took his bag and walked to the reception. Melinda, the lab receptionist, was still busy sorting through research paperwork. "Congratulations, Moose!" Melinda said, joyfully.

Not again. One of his fans.

"Thank you, Melinda. Don't mention it!"

Melinda passed the register for him to sign. Moose signed it and gave it back. As he was waiting for Melinda to sign it, he decided to take a look at the newspaper on the table. He could see today's date at the top. Moose read the headline.

And he read it again. No. It couldn't be. He scanned through the article, and then he did it again. No…

"Hey, Melinda," Moose called out, "Is this today's paper?"

"Yes, Moose. Why?" she replied.

Moose shook his head. "No, Melinda. Nothing." He kept the paper back on the table. He gave it one final glance.

Then, he turned around and walked out. His feet felt like lead, scraping along the ground. His head felt like lead too. He could still see the headlines in front of his eyes, like an imprint forever etched onto his mind. He closed his eyes, but the headline was still there.

12-YEAR-OLD BOY FROM ORPHANAGE KIDNAPPED ON LOLLIPOP AVENUE.

6

"Look, smile, relax. Look, smile, relax," Moose said to himself as he came out of the gray building. At his side was Sally.

"Great tip, don't you think, Moose? It's really going to help us in our next conversation," Sally said. It was their speech club's meeting today, and it had just finished.

Moose looked at Sally. He smiled and eased his shoulder down. Sally giggled.

"Yep, it works," Moose added, nodding his head. "It feels nice, doesn't it, to have a club like ours? A club where people actually understand the difficulty of speaking."

Sally nodded. "Sometimes, I wonder what we would do without it, Moose." Sally kept shaking her head, deep in thought. "The people here are so nice. They are just like us."

Sally looked at Moose. "And then there's the tips. Can't go wrong with the tips." Sally started saying, 'Look, smile, relax,' to herself over and over again. She smiled, happy with herself.

Moose had reached a small dark green car—his car. "OK, Sally. I need to go somewhere. Do you want me to drop you?"

Sally refused politely, flooding over in a deluge of 'no thank you' and 'I'll be fine'. She disappeared round the corner with that. Moose got into the car and started it. The dashboard was made of wood, and the seats had gotten a bit faint. A tall, lean 'tower' rose up from the middle of the two front seats, the gearbox. The steering wheel was thin too. It looked more like a large ring with two spokes and a disc in the center. Moose rubbed the wheel fondly. He stretched his back after he sat down, and felt the cushions caressing him. He loved his car. That was all he knew.

He drove along streets he knew since childhood. It was his usual path. After a few turns and twists, he reached his destination: a tall white building with a spire to the top. A clock made a circle on one face of the spire, its hands the color of bronze, its face yellow too. Moose felt chills run down his back. He always felt it, whenever he came to this place. In the space of the windows, dragons fought soldiers and royal women held doves in their hands. The stains were of the most beautiful colors. The huge oak doors stood amongst this holiness, doors that welcomed anyone in. It was the church, after all.

Moose glided closer, expecting to meet with the usually faded walls of the church. Instead, Moose had to rub his eyes and look twice. The walls were bright white, the color of clouds on a sunny day. Eyes wide, Moose looked around him. Men in yellow hard hats and fluorescent jackets rushed past Moose. Buckets of white paint stood every meter or so, and lean poles stiffened the sides of the church, scaffolding. Moose stepped into this land like a newcomer. Everything seemed… different.

He saw Sam standing near the entrance of the polished interiors of the church with a group of workers. Sam held a blueprint in his hands, and he was showing something to the construction crew. As soon as Sam saw Moose, he waved, smiling. "Oh, hello there, Moose! How's my employee of the month? All good?" He widened his smile at the end. Moose looked at Sam's irresistible smile, and, no matter how much he tried not to, he smiled back.

"What's all this, Sam?" Moose asked, looking around him.

"Just some renovations, Moose, Thought I would do something good, for once!" Sam laughed, trying to be modest. Moose felt like rolling his eyes. As if Sam was not doing enough.

Moose continued his interrogation. "But, why didn't you tell me about the renovations, Sam? You know me. I would have loved to know earlier. At least, you could have told me one word. I come to church every week."

Sam's smile still did not waver. It only grew wider. "Well, Moose, I thought I would make it a surprise. Who doesn't like surprises, right?" Sam laughed at the end. Moose smiled. This was the problem with Sam. When he laughs, you feel like laughing too. "Anyway, Moose, wouldn't want to keep you from praying. I will show you the way to the new temporary entrance."

Sam escorted him to the entrance and asked if he needed anything else (so kind). Moose stepped into the renovated hall, his lungs filling up with the smell of floor polish. He could smell the freshness of the pine wood and the marble statues from here. He sat down, still in awe at the large crystal dome of the church. The dome wasn't there before. The way it spiraled upwards and reflected bright colors onto the floor of the church was enough to ease Moose. Moose felt calm. He closed his eyes and entered the world that feels so much more peaceful than ours.

Moose didn't know how long he had been away. He opened his eyes and was blinded by the lack of light. It felt so much darker than it was before. The light on the ground had flown away to one side now, and shadows were cast here and there. Moose got up, looked at the altar one last time, and went out.

After looking around him and scanning the church's walls with some difficulty, Moose decided that everyone had left. Sam (and his smile) was nowhere to be found. A brick path rose before him, and he took it without a second thought. His feet were accustomed to the twists and turns of the path, and he was confident that his legs would take the same route even if he did not give them any instructions.

A brown, wooden building entered his vision. The building was small, and its windows were filled with dew. The roar of the fire that crackled in its chimney could be heard well out on the path. As Moose stepped in through the door, he felt like he was at his home. Well, he did come here often. The orphanage was like his own house.

The light inside was not switched on, and the only luminous object inside was the log fire. It might have been something about the dim surroundings, but his heart felt drained of joy. A young lady stood at the counter, and she looked up as Moose entered. Margherita, the young caretaker of the orphanage. She smiled at Moose, but it was not her usual, peppy smile. It was bent at the ends, and her brow, which was close together and low, did not match the show of happiness that her mouth tried to put up. Moose felt like breathing was getting harder. He breathed in deeply, but that seemed to make everything worse. It seemed that he was inhaling the melancholy atmosphere inside the orphanage too.

He tried to walk towards the fire and warm his hands. That's… that's when he saw the paper. It was half burned in its peaceful existence under one of the logs.

12-YEAR-OLD BOY FROM ORPHANAGE…

Moose could only see the first half of the headlines. The fire had taken away the rest. Moose swallowed hard. He looked at the spitting of the fire and thought about the boy. The worst thing was, he had seen the boy just a few days ago, on Halloween. The boy had gone trick-or-treating. Moose shivered. The boy had gone trick-or-treating to the stranger's house. The smile, the wave. Moose could remember it all. He shook his head, trying to forget.

Moose looked back at Margherita. He smiled again. She smiled back too, and they stood like that for a long time. Moose didn't know what to say. "Sorry," he finally said.

Margherita smiled at that too. "You don't have to be sorry, you know, Moose. It's OK." She kept nodding her head after that. It was a small movement, but her eyes looked less and less lost the more she did it.

Moose decided to try another question. "Where's Jack, Maggi?"

Margherita shook her head one last time, and replied, "Of course, he's in the playroom, with Sam."

Moose had known where Jack would be. Nevertheless, he thanked Maggi and neared the playroom.

When you think about a playroom you might think that it was one of those rooms with a lot of toys laying around and tiny children playing about. The orphanage's playroom definitely wasn't like that. It looked just like any normal living room, except for the huge number of chairs and sofas. There were so many chairs that it felt overwhelming.

Sadly, there weren't enough visitors to sit on them. Just like always, when Moose entered, he saw only Sam and a dozen or so kids. Sam was telling them a story and the kids were riveted by his narration. They didn't notice Moose come in, so he decided to stand by the doorframe, careful not to even breathe out a whisper that would disturb these children's precious story-telling time. He had to admit that even he was a bit caught up with the story. Sam definitely knew how to touch the children's hearts. He was a half-time pediatrician, after all.

But amongst this crowd, one child looked at Moose. He wore a blue tee, the color of the sea. His hair was wavy and was folded to one side. He wore black jeans, with sneakers. The sneakers were worn and wagged, but they weren't dirty. The boy ran to Moose and gave him a tight hug, like always. Then he hi-fived Moose.

"How are you doing, my Jack?" Moose asked, looking at the boy with eager eyes.

"Oh well. The usual, Uncle Moose. How are you?" Jack was looking at Moose with gleaming eyes.

"I am more than fine, Jack." Moose ruffled Jack's hair, just like he would for Timmy. Then, they continued listening to Sam's mighty narration of mighty tales.

Moose was sitting there at the edge of his seat, ears fixed to each and every syllable intonated by Sam. That was when he remembered. Oh no! He had forgotten. He had forgotten!

Moose jumped out of his seat. The kids all turned around to see what happened to their uncle. "Sorry, kids. Sorry, Sam. I really forgot to do something. I am so sorry." He looked one last time at the kids' faces, his eyes trying to apologize too. "Sorry! Uncle Moose will come some other day. Soon, uncle promises."

Some of the kids whined. Jack said, "It's OK, Uncle Moose. We understand."

"Yeah, tell him, Jack," Sam chorused. Then, he looked at Moose. "Don't worry, Moose. I'll take good care of the children."

Moose smiled. He knew Sam would. Of course, good old Sam, wasn't he? Moose left, relieved to know the kids weren't too sad.

Moose got into his car and drove back home as fast as he could. Well, as fast as he could, given the fact that he was the most careful driver he knew. He was the type of person who never likes to drive fast, the type of person who is careful when switching gears so that the gearbox wouldn't break. He was the type of person who sometimes hits reverse instead of hitting accelerate. He was the type of person who actually used the rear-view mirrors to park. He was a good driver.

After just a few minutes, Moose saw a gray house climb out of the horizon. It was a perfect square, and white-washed fences poked out of the edge of the garden. It looked just like any other building on the block, but to Moose, it meant something else. It was a place to wind down after a busy day of work. It was a place full of joy and happiness. It was home.

Moose parked his car in the small garage that mingled with the main house. He got out, a frown on his face. He nearly forgot his car keys inside. He chided himself, imagining the dire situation of being locked out of his own car. Rushing through the doorway, he called out to Timmy, "I am home, Tim Tim." Timmy rushed down the stairs, only to be caught in Moose's usual act of hair-ruffling. He didn't stop, no, he had to do something before that. A split second later, he was in the backyard.

In the middle of the small garden was a tree. Its trunk was wide and so strong that it filled observers' hearts with confidence and an odd sense of relief. Bright, shining apple earrings hung from the tree's head, and its base held onto the ground firmly like nature's hands. Moose walked closer and closer to him. With every step, his heart fell deeper and deeper into a state of peace. He patted the trunk. In the middle of the trunk, exactly in the center, was an imprint of seven hands.

Two of them came from his grandparents, and these were at the top.

Memories crashed into his mind. He was a young boy, playing on a swing that hung by the apple tree. His grandparents were pushing him, and all Moose had to do was sit and hold tight.

The swing had gone with time, but one thing from that day remained: the imprint. His grandparents, his parents, and Moose had all carved it at the same time.

He tried putting his hand on top of his grandfather's imprints. No, it wouldn't fit snugly. His hand was too small. He smiled. Big hand grandpa. That was what he used to call his grandfather. He tried to fit his hand on the next imprint, his father's. It wouldn't fit either. His hand was too small again. Even the imprint knew that Moose couldn't be like his father. His father was strong. Moose was weak. His father was brave. Moose, well, he wasn't. His father was very tall. Moose wasn't that tall. Then, his hand stroked his wife's imprints. He thought about her and all the moments they had together. Moose always had an amazing life. He was always the apple of everyone's eye. He smiled.

From all this happiness, finally, his thoughts came onto the kidnapped child. It was like coming from a garden of sheer beauty to a dry, bare, vile desert. He never, never, thought a child would get kidnapped from Lollipop Avenue. It was scary to know that there was a kidnapper in their own town. Moose thought about that day on Halloween when he had seen the boy, the kidnapped (Moose swallowed hardly) boy… for… for the last time. And he thought about where the boy stood. In front of the stranger's house. Moose swallowed hard again. He didn't know. Maybe he should suspect the stranger. The stranger did always have a nasty air around him. But then again, what if the stranger was innocent, what if Moose's mind was just being a bit too 'creative'?

Then, he thought about Sam. He didn't know why he thought of Sam, but he did. Sam was a nice guy. Moose had to admit that.

Moose looked at his stomach.

His gut didn't think so, apparently. His instincts told him there was something, something, about Sam. Moose didn't know what it was. Moose didn't like to think ill about anyone. He liked to think that maybe, he was just a bit jealous of Sam. But something told Moose not to ignore his gut feeling. He shook his head, not knowing what to think, let alone know what to do.

He patted the tree's trunk. At least his dear tree was listening to this. At least, he had someone to talk to about this. He stood there for some time, stroking the tree's brown trunk, careful not to move his hand down too hard. That was when something bright and green caught his eye. He looked closer to the thing on the ground and, realizing what it was, he ran to get the garden scissors.

He sat down on the ground, close to the weed, a gigantic scissor in one hand. The weed twisted around the base of the tree in its crooked manner. It was long, but it only occupied a small space on the ground. He had to cut the weed. He had to. He opened the scissor up, exposing sharp blades. He aligned it with the neck of the weed and started counting down. Three… he wasn't going to let the weed hurt his tree… Two… but the weed was a living thing, wasn't it? Should he cut it? It deserved a place in the world. Moose looked at the weed once again. It looked so small. How could such a small plant really hurt his tree? No, he wasn't going to cut it. By the time Moose reached 1 in his head, he had already made up his mind. He put the scissor down. *CLANK*.

7

Moose opened his eyes and gasped. He rose up at lightning speed, turned, and grabbed the jug of water by his bedside table. *GLUG, GLUG, GLUG.* He kept the jar back, wiped his mouth with the back of the sleeve of his pajamas, and stared at the white wall of his bedroom. He thought about what he had seen in the nightmare. He was little Moose, the Moose that went to school, and the Moose that wore a school uniform. He thought about the bullies. The bullies had come to him after school, a gang of them altogether. They had pushed him, taken all his food. When he pleaded with them to stop, they kicked him in the stomach. He looked at his stomach. He could feel the blow. He rubbed his stomach, still in his trance.

He had decided to tell the teacher. But the teacher wouldn't believe him, no matter how much he showed his bruises. Nobody would. She blamed Moose. For what, Moose didn't know. Moose looked at the wall. Nobody would remember a dream so clearly unless it was their own life.

Moose got up from the bed. He climbed down the stairs to the living room and then directed himself to the backyard. He went to his tree and stood there for some time. He breathed in the clean, fresh air, and his lungs felt relaxed. He eased his shoulders and closed his eyes, listening to the birdsong. Then, patting the tree trunk to mark his attendance, he left, this time in the direction of the kitchen. He entered. Happily, he got out some bread and chocolate spread. It was an unconscious action, for Moose was still stuck in his dream. He spread the chocolate all over the piece of bread. After he finished, he took a look at it. No, not enough. He took another spoon of chocolate, and he spread it over the bread once more. He looked at them again. No, not enough. Not enough. He turned the piece over and applied the spread on this side as well. He kept it on the table, admiring his masterpiece. It looked beautiful, a chocolate lover's delight! His mouth watered, and his stomach rumbled.

He took it in his hands, his mind filled only with the thought of savoring it.

Just then, a siren waffled through the air. *BEEP BOP. BEEP BOP. BEEP BOP.* It felt a bit doozy to hear a siren on Lollipop Avenue. The town was usually quiet, the birds its only siren. But now, everything had changed, hadn't it? He looked back at the toast and put it closer to his eyes, admiring it. The siren stopped, and all was calm again as Moose decided to take the first bite. He put it closer to his mouth, opened it, and…

DING DONG. Moose froze just as he was about to devour the chocolate bread. He looked at the front door, his eyebrows raised. Who would come to meet Moose in the morning? He looked at the clock—six o'clock. He inched to the front door, still a bit quizzical. He opened it.

There on the front mat stood a man of broad shoulders and a round tummy. He wore a blue hat with a golden badge at the center. The same badge hung from his blue shirt pocket, and

Moose could see the tiny glimmer of a gun's metallic end in one of the brown holders on the man's belt.

As if it wasn't obvious, the man held up the badge, unfurled his serious lips, and said, "Police."

Moose tried to smile at him, eyebrows still raised. Why would a policeman come to his house? "Good… good morning, sir. Is there something… something I can help you with?" Moose asked, wiping the beads of sweat on his forehead.

"Are you Mr Moosehorn Roosevelt?" the policeman asked.

"Yes, sir. I am… My name is Moose."

The policeman gave a slit-eye look at Moose and then looked at some papers in his hands. "Well, Mr Roosevelt. We got some… uh, complaints. We need you to come with us."

Moose smiled. The policeman had come to ask for a favor. "No problem, sir! I am more than happy to help you. Just let me change my clothes and I am coming."

The policeman eyed Moose again, stroking his chin. "No, sir. We don't need help. We got a complaint. About you. We need you to come to the station for an interrogation."

What.

Moose looked at the policeman again. A complaint… against him? For what? Why? Moose gripped the door handle tighter. "Sir… si—"

"Mr Roosevelt, please come with us. It will just be a uhm,"—the policeman looked at Moose, thinking for the right word—"*short* interrogation. Now, do you want to inform someone that you are leaving?"

Moose looked at the policeman for some time, not uttering a word.

"Sir, do you want to tell someone that you will be away for some time?" the policeman asked again, impatience snaking into his voice.

Moose nodded. He turned back and stood there like that, not knowing what to do. Then, he trudged upstairs to Timmy's room. He stepped in.

Timmy opened his eyes on hearing the creak of the door. He gave Moose a smile, but then he realized that his father wasn't smiling, and his face turned more worried. "What is it, Dad?"

"Timmy, I have to go."

Timmy pulled the sheets over and pulled himself straight. "Where, Dad? Where are you going?"

"Timmy, don't worry! Daddy's just going to the police station. I'll be back before you know it." Moose tried to cheer up. He didn't want Timmy to be sad.

Timmy's eyes were fixed on his father's. His mouth gaped open. "Why, Dad?"

"Well,"—Moose paused, thinking about what to say— "just for an interview, Timmy. They want to ask Daddy some questions. That's all. Now you be a good boy and go to bed."

Moose thought about the policeman and his impatience, and decided he had to get going. He climbed down the stairs with his head held low. Him, going to a police station. He never thought that likely. He looked up with a frown at the policeman. The policeman waited for him to step out as if he wanted to make sure Moose didn't run away. Moose stepped out, and the policeman walked right behind him.

Suddenly, he heard a thundering overhead. Someone was rushing through the floorboards above. And then, there Timmy was, standing by the doorframe. He held the frame, covering half of his face. He looked at Moose and the policeman with only one eye.

"Oh, Timmy. Why did you come down? Daddy is going to be back soon, isn't he?"

Timmy just stood there, looking at Moose. Moose glanced at the policeman, a bit scared that he would become impatient again. However, the policeman took off his hat and went near Timmy. He put his hand on Timmy's shoulder, and said, "Hey, kiddo. We were going to bring Daddy back home soon. Don't cha worry."

Timmy nodded, a finger pulling anxiously at the side of his lips. He looked at the policeman for some time, then looked at Moose to know if it was true. Moose put up a smile.

"Now, go upstairs, Timmy. Lock the door. Don't forget," Moose said.

The policeman took Moose up the drive to the police car parked in the front. It was just a normal sedan, made for the quiet life at Lollipop Avenue. The policeman went with Moose till he entered, and he then got in himself. He started the siren. *BEEP BOP, BEEP BOP, BEEP BOP.*

Moose looked out through his window. People started coming out now, surprised to hear a siren in their small town. Moose himself had only heard the siren a couple of times in his long stay at Lollipop Avenue. Moose looked at the faces of all the people who were coming out, and they looked back at him, too. Some had their hands on their mouth. Others were shaking their heads. Moose looked at them, trying to tell them he hadn't done anything wrong with his eyes. They didn't understand, they just kept shaking their heads. Nobody understood Moose. And amongst these people was Sally. She stood there, aghast. She blinked a few times, trying to make sure that this was the reality she knew and lived in. Her eyes looked… saddening. To Moose, it felt like they was asking him why he had betrayed her. Why? Why? The car started, and it drove slowly through the throng of people. It drove too slowly. Moose couldn't escape from the gloom as fast as he would have liked to.

And as he made his way out of the lot, he thought about his sandwich, still on his kitchen table. He hadn't even taken a bite. He looked out of the window, not knowing whether it was the rain or his tears that made everything go blurry.

8

Moose thought about what had happened back at the police station. He thought about how they had cuffed Moose, as if he was already a criminal. He thought about how they had taken him to the room, the white room with a plain table in the middle. They had told him to sit, and they had put a black device in the middle of the desk. Some kind of recorder that beeped every five minutes. They had asked Moose a lot of questions. A lot. The policeman that had taken him to the station had not been there. In his place was another cop, a cop with a thick mustache. The cop threatened to put him in a cell if he didn't speak up.

Moose thought about how he had told them it wasn't him. "No, sir. I... I didn't do it. I wouldn't kidnap anybody. A child, never. Why don't you believe me?" As he said that, the cop had pounded the table with his fist. Moose still remembered how hard the cop clenched his mouth. You could see the nerves pulsing in his neck. He told Moose about how the police had gotten a complaint against Moose. "I know you are the kidnapper. I know it. Come on, accept it! Accept IT!" He kept questioning Moose for a long time. He had sighed after every one of Moose's answers. Then, in the end, he had barged out of the door without telling Moose anything, leaving only a table overturned in his anger.

Moose sat there for a long time until the policeman returned. "Hello, sonny. We know you are a criminal. You think you can fool us, huh? We'll catch you one day. Right, boys?" Then, he and his comrades had laughed. He opened Moose's cuffs and pushed him out through the front door. And now he here was, the criminal.

The rain was pattering down on Moose without mercy, but Moose didn't care. He was a criminal, wasn't he? The streets were a one-man's storm, a sea without anybody brave enough to brave it. He walked alone, his shirt shot by the drops that fell from the sky. He kept his head down, afraid that someone would see his face. The shadows were his only refuge as he tried to drown himself in its comfort.

He looked at the gray pavement, which was drenched in the same gray water. The sky looked gray, and the sun shined gray light all over the street. The gray trees swayed with the gray wind.

Everything was gray…

He felt cold. He hugged himself to keep himself warm. His teeth chattered. His hands shivered. But he decided to keep walking. Anyway, who would care if he was cold?

As he walked across the street, his feet hit the puddles. *BLING, BLING, BLING, BLING.*

PING! Moose looked at his phone. There was a message. From George.

He tried to peer into the glass of the phone, but the rain drops made that harder too.

"Guess who got the employee-of-month award!" the message said.

It had been one month since Moose had last received the award. It felt joyous and pleasing to hear that he had got the award this month as well. At least, there was some light amid all this darkness, Moose thought. The twitches of a smile formed on his face. *PING!* A second message from George. It must be a 'congratulations' message. Moose looked at it, and as he read it, he stopped walking.

"Sam got it!" the message said, followed by a smiling emoji.

'Sam got it,' Moose thought. 'Sam?'

Moose looked at the message again.

'Sam, Sam, Sam. It was always Sam now, wasn't it?' Moose kicked a pebble lying on the street. 'Sam. Why is it always Sam? Why?'

Sam's smile, his face, his behavior, Moose could smell a rat. But who would listen to him? Moose was just a kidnapper. He wasn't someone to believe, was he? Moose pushed his hands into his pockets. He could already hear his colleagues laughing at him for blaming Sam. No. Moose wasn't going to tell anyone anything. He didn't want to be laughed at anymore.

Moose looked to his sides and realized that he was nearing his house. He sighed. Nothing felt the same again. He didn't feel happy to be back home.

He saw Sally. She was on her front lawn, hovering over a group of cacti that she was tending. Moose's footsteps made her turn to his side. Moose waved at Sally, smiling for the first time that day. Or so it seemed.

Sally didn't wave back. She looked to her sides, trying to see if anyone was watching. Then, she looked at Moose and waved. But it wasn't like the usual. Her mouth was screwed in a serious face. Then, she went back to her cacti.

Moose stepped closer to her garden fence. "Sally!" he called out.

No response. Sally kept her face glued to her cactus.

Moose's face waned. No, Sally must not have heard him. Yes, that was it. Moose called out again, a bit louder, "Sally!"

Sally stopped cutting the cactus spines and froze. She was still looking in the direction of the cactus, but she had her face deep in thought. Then, suddenly, she dropped her scissors and spades on the floor, got up, and rushed to the front door of her house. She got in. *BANG.* The door was shut.

Moose could hear the lock being fastened. Once. Twice.

He heard a rattling as if the chain of the door was also being put up.

The first blind was drawn down. And the second. And the third.

"Sally…"

Moose kept his eyes fixed on the door. For some time, he stood there, shoulders limp and chin down. He kept staring at the door. Sally… Sally didn't believe him? Sally?

He shook his head. He turned around and sat down on the floor. He didn't think about how wet it was. And then, all of a sudden, the sadness, the sadness burst. He put his head in his hand. He was the criminal. He was the criminal. No. No…

And then, he wept.

9

Moose rose from his bed, muscles stiff. He smacked his lips, only to taste the bitterness of his own tears. He didn't know how he had gotten back home, but he had. He huffed and puffed down the stairs.

He walked to the front door, his mind bogged down by thought after thought. He put his hand on the handle, but he didn't open the door. Instead, he just stood there, staring at the eyehole without really seeing anything. He thought about yesterday. He thought about Sally. Moose thought about all the things going wrong in his life. He sighed. Realizing that he was standing in the middle of the doorway like a fish gone cold, he regained his senses and pulled the door inwards. He stepped out and looked at the newspaper laying on the ground.

His eyes widened. He dropped down and grabbed the paper, noticing the words in bold at the top.

A SECOND CHILD GOES MISSING ON LOLLIPOP AVENUE.

Moose couldn't blink. He fell onto their sofa, never daring to take his eyes off the article. He read the piece, and then he read it again. He read all the gruesome details. But those didn't hit him like the boy in the picture. He looked at the boy. He would recognize that face anywhere. Who wouldn't recognize that blue tee, or the windswept black hair?

Jack.

He looked at the smiling face of Jack in the picture, and he wondered if the face was still smiling. He kept the paper down, and thought about who would do such a thing. Who was this monster?

He thought about all the times he had spent with Jack together. He thought about all the people at the orphanage who were crying now. Like a collage, the images played out in his mind's eye as he stared at the front wall. He couldn't stop thinking.

Then, suddenly, he kept the paper down and got up. He climbed up the stairs again. Pushing the door gently, he crept into Timmy's room. Timmy was bundled up under the sheets, sleeping on his sides, away from Moose. Moose tiptoed next to the bed and sat down, trying his best not to make a ruckus. CREAK, the bed went. He looked at Timmy's face. Had Timmy woken up from the sound?

He exhaled. Timmy hadn't. Moose put his hand on Timmy's shoulder. Wishing just to enjoy the moment, he stroked Timmy's hair, careful to be as gentle as a feather. Wishing to enjoy it a little more, he bent down and kissed Timmy on the head. Ah. He would never forget that moment. It felt good to have his Timmy next to him. His heart felt light and warm.

His mind strolled off, suddenly, to Jack…

Jack was Timmy's age…

Moose gulped. What if? What if Timmy also—Moose cut his own thoughts. No. Nothing would happen to his bundle of joy. Moose looked out from the window at the nearby houses, thinking about the kidnapper that was out there, somewhere.

Who would really do such a thing?

Moose got up, slowly at first, but fixing his mind, he got out of the room as fast as he could.

Should he really suspect Sam?

Moose thundered down the stairs and bolted to the door. He pulled it open so fast that his hand slipped from the handle and the door banged on the wall. But he didn't stop.

Was Sam the kidnapper?

He had to know. Moose walked with purposeful strides. The sun shone brightly on his pajamas. He threw open the front gate and turned to the left. His pace quickened the closer he got.

At the end of the road, he saw the sign. Moose knew where he had to go. He looked at the sign, pointing to the right.

HANDSOME MANOR.

10

Moose was walking as fast as he could now. He was running and walking at the same time. He would find out today. He would find the answers.

As he came closer and closer to the gate, he saw that it was wide open. That was… unusual. Moose shrugged it off. It was morning, and the mailman usually came around by this time. It was probably just open for him.

Moose was now just a few feet away from the metal rods of the gate. Just before he put his feet in, he looked to the sides. Was the guard around anywhere, that rude, little guard? Seeing no one, Moose slipped in without hesitation.

He took powerful strides. And then he froze.

He saw the guard, just inches to his right. The guard was playing with a dog, Frisbee in hand.

Moose unfroze his legs. He took a step, then stopped. He looked at the guard. The guard hadn't noticed. Then, Moose took another step, his eyes still fixed on the guard and the dog. He took a third step, and a fourth, and another, and another. Soon, he was back at his original pace. His feet were pointing to the front door of the house. He knew where he had to go.

As he galloped along, his eyes fell on the top of the building by mistake. He was, as always, captivated by its beauty. All the windows looked dark, except one on the far right. It was illuminated by an orange light. Why there was a light in the morning, Moose didn't know. But Moose wasn't going to let something as silly as a yellow light dissipate his anger. With renewed determination, he got his rage back as he thought of Jack, as he thought of why he had come here.

He barged up the front steps and rang (banged) the doorbell. He kept pressing it for some time, more out of anger than reason.

Moose could hear footsteps. It came from the top, and then he could hear it straight ahead.

The lock opened and Sam came out. He was wearing a bright yellow raincoat, with blue shoe covers over his feet. Moose looked at his hand. He held a test tube. Oh, typical Sam. Working on his medicines from home, even on a weekend. Poor guy, Moose thought. Sam was smiling, but one by one, his facial features changed to express shock. His eyebrows went up to his forehead. His eyes widened. A small gap formed in between his lips. His spectacle dropped down to the edge of his nose. Then, all the features went back to normal, and Sam smiled ever wider.

"Moose? This is quite a surprise," Sam said, waiting for Moose to say something. He scanned Moose from head to toe, trying to stifle a laugh. His eyes returned to Moose. He gave a chuckle. "Nice PJs, Moose."

Moose looked at himself. He tried to smile, but he could feel his cheeks getting hot. He gave Sam an apologetic look.

"Seems you were in quite a," Sam said, emphasizing the last word, "*hurry*." Sam's smile dimmed a little at the end as if he was expecting a reply. "Come on, what is it, Moose? You can always tell me."

Moose froze, for real this time. He hadn't thought about what he would tell Sam. He thought his eyes might have been bulging because Sam seemed a bit worried for a moment. Moose searched for words. Come on. Excuses, excuses, excuses. Nothing came to mind. Then, in his scramble, he found an escape route. He got back his anger and snapped, "Can I come in, Sam? Let's talk inside."

Sam looked over his shoulder to the inside of his house. He turned back to Moose and grinned. "Why don't we talk near the benches outside, Moose? The children, you know, have done it on the floor."

Moose nodded, his anger easing.

Sam got out and closed the door behind him. He walked first and Moose followed. They were going somewhere to the side of the manor. As they were walking, Moose decided to ask Sam about something that was bothering him.

"Hey, Sam. Why are you wearing a raincoat?"

Sam chuckled, a bit slowly. "Well, blame me for believing the weather guy when he said it's going to rain." He looked back at Moose, to see if he had smiled too. Now, under the sun, Moose could see the patches of black under Sam's eyes. Even as Sam smiled, wrinkles of lethargy creased themselves onto his face. Seeing Sam trudge along, shoulders a bit hunched, he couldn't but wonder if Sam had seen his bed yesterday.

The more they walked, the more Moose's suspicion wore away. Sam was working from home, and he seemed like he was working all the time. Could a person like this…?

Before Moose could finish his thoughts, his focus shifted to Sam, who made himself comfortable on a wooden bench overlooking the river to the side of the Handsome Manor. He was looking at Moose, waiting for him to sit down as well.

Moose sat down, trying to ease his shoulders and relax. He couldn't.

He had sat at the edge of the bench. He looked at Sam. Without a glance at anything else, Sam's eyes were trained on the waterbed. Moose tried to guess what Sam was thinking of now. But, to Moose's immense disappointment, Sam's face didn't even give a single clue.

Moose decided to look at the waterbed too. He had nothing better to do, anyway. Time passed. Five minutes. Then ten. Moose started to play with his fingers, restless.

Finally, Sam said, "I know why you are here, Moose."

Moose looked at Sam so fast that he thought he had broken his neck. Did Sam know? What was he thinking now? Was he going to do something bad to him? Moose waited for the next words.

"It's about the kidnap, isn't it?" Sam said. His eyes were still fixed on the river.

How did he know? No. Moose's mind was racing now. He could feel his stomach churning and his heart twisting. On one side, his mind was paralyzed with fear. On the other, his mind was accelerating with excitement. He might not live to see another day. But at least he would know if his gut was right or wrong before that happened.

Moose couldn't take it any longer. "How do you—" Moose realized his voice was just a croak. Mustering up the loudness of his voice, he asked again, "How do you know, Sam?"

Sam smiled, never even taking his eyes off the water once. "Well, it was a sad kidnap, wasn't it?"

Moose waited for Sam to continue, but he didn't. Had Moose heard Sam correctly? Was Sam actually… sad about his own kidnap? Moose shook his head. Was his hearing fine?

Now, Sam looked at Moose. His face was rock solid, set in a tightly sad look. He continued, "Well, Moose, I feel sorry for the kid. Just like you, I didn't see it coming."

OK. Moose's shoulders dropped. Now he knew where Sam was going. He wasn't confessing. He was just trying to console Moose. Moose leaned back, his mind filled to the brim with questions. And he realized he wasn't going to find their answers anytime soon.

"Might have been the stranger," Sam added. "You never know. I always, you know, sensed something wrong in him."

Moose thought about that. He had seen the first kidnapped child near the stranger's house, hadn't he? In Halloween? Moose looked down at the grass. Could he have stopped the child from getting kidnapped? Maybe…

Sam looked at Moose and patted him on the back. "It's OK, Moose. It's OK."

Not for the first time that day, the two sat motionlessly, Sam's hand still on Moose's shoulder. Then, Sam got up. "Moose, we can't do anything about it, can we? About the kidnap? Stop thinking about it. It isn't going to do you any good."

And with that, it was over. "See you at the office, Moose," Sam said, trying to act jolly. His face still seemed a bit sad nevertheless.

Moose waited until Sam had walked to the edge of the mansion and then vanished through the turning. Then, he looked at the river and thought. Thought about what to do.

Thought about who to blame. Sam had seemed innocent. Maybe he was innocent, Moose thought.

Moose looked up at the sky. Or maybe Sam wasn't. After all, a criminal never confesses.

<h1 style="text-align:center">11</h1>

Moose stared at the blank supplements' sales report, a plain white document on his computer. He sighed. He fidgeted with the badges on his lanyard and leaned back on his office chair. He tried closing his eyes, but all he could see in the darkness was the face of all the children. He opened his eyes, more out of fear than anything else. He didn't want to think about it. He turned his focus back to the report. He hovered his hands over the white keyboard, but before he had typed a single letter, he glanced at the newspaper to his side, at the little face at the side. And then his hand froze again.

Shaking his head, he tried to push his mind back to the sales report. The sales report, Moose, the sales report, he kept telling himself. He looked at the sheet of medical data in front of his keyboard and entered the first figure. £31,000.

He froze again. £31, 000. 31. 31 October.

Halloween.

The day when he had seen the first kidnapped child for the last time.

Moose slumped in his chair, head in hand, leaning sideways and thinking. He looked to his sides, at the countless empty chairs, and he wondered where all his friends were. He looked down at the ground. He didn't have anybody. Not a soul.

Laughter echoed across the silent hall. Moose looked up, ears on alert. Who on Earth was so happy? He saw George and Sam coming in together through the entrance. Moose looked at them. Sam was telling something to George, gesturing with his hands, and George was crying with joy. 'How could someone… be… so, so, so…' Moose struggled to find the right word.

George looked at Moose just as he was about to pass him and then turned his head away, wrinkling his nose. He acted like Moose was invisible. Just a no one.

Sam said his trademark greeting. "Howdy, Moose. How's it going?"

Sam waited for a response. Seeing Moose's drooping face, he asked, "You OK, Moose? Still thinking about the kidnap?" Moose didn't answer, but maybe his posture gave his heart away. Sam seemed to know exactly what he was thinking. "Don't you worry, Moose. It's not in our hands. What can we do?"

"Moosehorn." Moose looked at the person who had called him by his full name. It was Melinda, the lab receptionist.

"The boss is calling you, Moose. Says he wants to talk with you," Melinda said.

Moose's eyebrows were furrowed in thought. Why did Boss call me? As Moose made his way to Mr Riley's office, Moose thought about getting a salary raise. Ah, that would be great, Moose thought, moving his jaws up to form a smile.

He knocked on the door.

"Come in."

Moose's eyebrows furrowed deeper. There was something about the 'come in' that felt wrong to Moose. Something.

Moose went in, a bit reluctant to enter. He walked and took a seat opposite Mr Riley. Mr Riley was wearing his oversized blazer, with a perfectly ironed shirt. As soon as Moose sat down, Mr Riley closed his computer, put his locked hands on the table, and looked at Moose with his piercing eyes. Moose tried to smile, like always. Mr Riley didn't.

"Well, I will cut to the chase, Moose. That way, it's better for both of us," Mr Riley said.

Moose just looked at Mr Riley. Moose's hands were shaking, and he tried to hide them from the Boss' keen eyes.

"What is happening to you, Moose?"

Moose looked at the table, not knowing what to say. He could feel the heat of the Boss's gaze on his forehead.

"What is happening to you, Moose?" the Boss asked again.

"Your sales have been going down. DOWN!" He was bellowing now.

Moose still had his eyes down. Some seconds passed like that, and the Boss just stared at Moose.

He waited for an answer. Finally, with a puff, he continued. "You know what, Moose? Leave the sales. I am not going to talk about it."

"I received a complaint about you. People don't want to work with… with… uhm… a *kidnapper*." The Boss said the last words with such confidence that Moose's face shot up, and he looked at the boss with widened eyes.

"Boss, do you really think that? Do you…" Moose's feeble voice faded off. "Do you really think I am… a kidnapper?" He looked at the boss without taking his eyes off him. Moose's lips twitched. His whole body was shaking.

"No, Moose. I would not," the boss said, his face stone-cold and hard. It did not betray even a single emotion. "Anyway, Moose, a small break will do you only good," he continued. Moose stared at the boss, the open slit in his mouth growing. A break?

The boss looked at Moose's shocked face. Then, he added, "Don't worry, Moose. It's just a small leave from work. Go do something you love. Go do fishing!" He laughed at the end, but his laugh was too long. The pitch of the laugh was all wrong. It seemed terribly fake. Seeing that Moose wasn't smiling, the boss stopped laughing and adjusted his tie. He came back to his old position all suddenly.

In an instant, Mr Riley put his hand inside one of the lab drawers and pulled out a set of papers. He cleared his throat. "Moose, now, sign this." Moose looked at the red pen for some time. He took it. For some time, he looked at his own hand too. The pen was wobbling. His hand was shaking. The boss looked at it too, transfixed.

Moose put the pen to the paper and signed it. Each and every single page. One by one by one. His sign appeared haphazard because of the state of his hand and the state of his mind. He didn't care. Would any man care when he was signing his own death will?

Before Moose put the last sign, he stopped and thought about all the good times he had. He thought about getting to be the employee of the month. He could hear the claps in his mind. And then, he put the last sign. As he finished, a single drop fell from his eyes and onto the paper, right onto where he had left the pen. The boss looked at it too. But then, he looked away, pretending not to have seen it.

Moose put the pen down, screeched the chair back, and ran out the door. "Moose…" the boss called out. But Moose didn't stop. He waited till the door closed behind him, and then he stood right there. Right there in front of the door. He closed his eyes. He bit his lip. He didn't want to cry. No. He didn't want to cry.

His whole world was crashing down. And so was he.

<h1 style="text-align:center">12</h1>

Moose was soaked. Water dripped from his shirt and pants. He let it drip. Who would care if he was wet? This was the second time he was walking home like this, the second time he had his head drooped down like this. He didn't feel like looking up. He would keep his head down... forever. He didn't want to raise it anymore.

The top button of his shirt was undone, and he held his tie in his hanging hands. A fallen angel. A hated criminal. A stranger. But it wasn't always like that, was it? It wasn't always like that. It was lovely—Moose, the hero; Moose, the kind neighbor; Moose, the best employee. He wiped his face. How, how could he have crashed like this? His lungs felt like they were stuck. He couldn't breathe.

No. He didn't *want* to breathe.

Everyone was against him. He looked up. Even the weather. *CRACKLE. CRACKLE. CRACKLE.* As soon as he was done thinking, the rain started falling with greater rage.

When it rains, it pours. It was true, wasn't it?

And it was really pouring now. When he thought of little Timmy at home, all he could feel in his chest was a churning. His mind was torn. His heart stopped pounding. What if he couldn't feed Timmy anymore? Or send him to school? He thought about Timmy sitting at home, lonely and hungry. He thought about what they would do to eat supper. And he felt, for the first time, like he could never climb back up. He couldn't. He couldn't…

He shook his head to get him back to life and looked around him. He looked at the house on the corner for some time, his house, deciding if he should go in or not. But where else could he go? He eyed the empty road, and then tramped up to his door.

As he went by, he noticed a yellow paper blaring out of the mailbox. He knew. He knew what it was. And he knew he would never be able to pay it. The mortgage. The bank. He reached for it, opened the mailbox, and took it out. He looked at the front page, wincing. Not because there was anything on it, but because he knew what was inside it. And he knew he was never going to be able to pay it now.

He went to the front door and rang the bell. He looked at the letters once more. Then, he looked away. No. He didn't want to open them just yet.

As the seconds passed into minutes, he wondered where Timmy was. Why was Timmy taking so long? He tried the door, not expecting it to budge one bit. But it did. Not again, Moose thought. Timmy must have forgotten to lock the door when he went to the backyard.

He stepped into the living room. "Timmy, I'm home!" he shouted out. No reply. Not that he thought Timmy would hear him from the backyard.

His eye couldn't leave the letters. He looked at it once more.

He sighed. Someday, he would have to open it. It was not like he could choose to run away. He put his hand, slowly, into the letter and tried to grab its paper, but all he could catch was thin air. He peeked inside the mail. If there wasn't any paper, what was inside?

He put his hand in whole and caught hold of something. Something smooth and cool to the touch. He pulled it out. They were…

… photos? There were three of them in it. He looked at the first one.

It was a picture of Timmy eating his cereals, smiling.

The clarity, the resolution… Moose took a glance at the kitchen window. Did someone take Timmy's picture from his own backyard?

He looked at the second picture, heart thumping. It was Timmy again. Only this time, he was in his room upstairs. The photo began to crinkle because of Moose's strong grip on it. The ends of his fingers turned white.

He looked at the last picture. This time, it wasn't Timmy's.

It was a painted picture. A man in a red-and-yellow jester's costume was holding a flute to his mouth, delighting his fingers over the instrument. Behind him, children were lining up to hear his song.

The Pied Piper of Hamelin.

Moose looked at the kids again. They were in a trance, not even in control of their own body. The Piper was smiling his crooked smile, his nose pointing forward to doom. His eyes were like slits of deceit. As Moose scanned the picture, he noticed something written on the back. He flipped the picture around, to see a yellow background and two words in blood-red ink.

YOU'RE NEXT.

Moose's eyes were transfixed on those two words. The dark color. The sadist texture. The way it crooked here and there.

Below the words was a white flute, holes endlessly deep and morose spanning its front, with a black snake coiled tightly around it. The snake around the Piper's rod seemed to fixate on Moose's eyes with an intensity so strong that it sucked out all the dreadful, intolerable, maddening guilt and misery in him. Moose kept the pictures down, but the snake's questioning eyes didn't leave his vision. It was like his worst nightmares. Someone was—Moose swallowed—targeting Timmy.

Timmy?

Moose rushed from the living room and jolted the backyard door open. He looked out, not seeing his son anywhere.

He ran upstairs. *TICK TOCK TICK. TICK TOCK TICK. TICK TOCK TICK.* The sound of the grandfather clock boomed across the silent house. Moose leaped across the floorboards. He tossed aside vacant chairs. He pushed the toys out of the way.

He opened the door to Timmy's room, his heart stopping. "Timmy…" he called out.

Timmy wasn't there.

13

"Timmy? Timmy?" Moose was going to every room now. Where was Timmy? He must be here somewhere.

Moose checked the attic. He checked the kitchen and the bathroom. He couldn't find Timmy anywhere. He rubbed his forehead with his palm. Where was Timmy? Where would he search? Suddenly, he got an idea. He knew the only place Timmy could be.

He rushed out of the front door. People stared at him, but he didn't care. He turned the corner to Handsome Manor. His feet were running on their own now, and his eyes followed the roads without him telling them to.

He turned around and saw a bicycle and a boy coming to him. That didn't stop him. But it did. When he saw the boy holding the cycle, it did. Moose's shoulders relaxed. His eyes became loose, and his eyebrows eased.

It was Timmy. Timmy was safe! Timmy had probably just gone to Sam's house, just like his hunch told him.

But, Timmy had gone to… Sam's house. Sam's house. Moose stared at Timmy, and for a second, he thought about the face on the cards. The Pied Piper. The photos with Timmy on them. It was close. Timmy could have been… could have been… Moose couldn't get the word out… kid… kid…

kidnapped. How many times had he told Timmy about Sam? Didn't he know he had to listen to his father?

Well. He would have to *make* him know. Moose took strong strides toward Timmy. He walked with purpose, fists held tight. Timmy smiled, just seeing his father now. Moose came to a halt in front of his son.

"Where were you, Timmy?" he interrogated.

Timmy, his usual, happy, cheerful self, replied, "I was at Uncle Sam's house, Daddy."

Timmy raised his hands up to reveal two things. "Look, Daddy. Here's what Uncle Sam gave me!" Moose took a glance at the poster and the pen.

COME ON NOW. IT'S TIME TO ACT, SING, AND LAUGH! These words were written out at the bottom in bold on Sam's poster. Timmy said, "Daddy, Uncle Sam's going to host this very large musical club with lots and lots of…"

Moose's eyes didn't leave the vicinity of the poster. Timmy was at Sam's, Moose thought. At *Sam's.*

"… and they have this flute concert ready for September, and all these famous conductors are going to be there, and—"

"—give the poster to me, TIMMY!" Moose barked. "And the PEN!"

Timmy looked at Moose's eyes for some time. His mouth hung open. He didn't blink. He placed the poster onto his father's outstretched hand and put the pen on top of it, his eyes looking up at Moose the whole time.

As soon as that was done, Moose leaped for Timmy's hand. With a strong grip on his wrist, he pulled Timmy back home. Timmy followed, his feet screeching on the ground. Nobody spoke.

Moose got inside the house and banged the door shut.

"Timmy, do you know how DANGEROUS that was?"

Timmy looked at Moose. His face was pale.

"DO YOU KNOW HOW DANGEROUS SAM IS, TIMMY?" Moose thundered on. He looked at Timmy, waiting for a response. None came.

Moose threw the blackmail letter over the tabletop at his son. Some of the pictures skidded and fell onto the floor. Timmy bent down and picked them up.

He looked at it for some time. "Daddy, but how do you know Uncle Sam took these?"

Moose's eyes flashed onto Timmy. "Sam, Sam, SAM! 'Uncle' Sam, is he?"

Moose's anger scanned the table with mad eyes. Moose grabbed Timmy's poster. *RIIIIPPPP.* Seeing the pen, he took it and fired it at the wall. "Go to your room, Timmy! NOW! YOU'RE GROUNDED!"

Timmy stepped back, his hands out in front of him. Tears formed in his eyes. His face was full of fear. Pure fear. For the first time, he seemed scared. Scared of his own father.

Then, he turned and ran back, wiping his face with his sleeves. Moose's anger dropped down, and he ran behind Timmy. "Timmy!" Timmy didn't stop. He ran into his room. Before closing the door, Timmy held a card up. "You're just jealous of Sam! This, this was a card I made for you." Timmy showed the card, and over his tears, he tore it. He looked at Moose, his whole face shivering. "I hate you, Dad! I hate you!"

BANG. Timmy slammed the door. Moose stared at the now-closed door, dumbfounded. He didn't understand what had just happened. But he did understand one thing.

Not even his own son believed him.

Moose fell to his knees. He took the pieces of the ripped Father's Day card in both hands. He cupped his hands, holding the cards as he would something precious. He felt its soft texture.

He pinched himself. No, he told himself. Not now. He closed his eyes, forcing his tears to stay back. Not now. No.

He just wanted to be a good father. For once, he wanted to do something good, something his son would be proud of. *I hate you, Dad.* Those words echoed in his mind. He just wanted to do something good. Something good.

Nobody believed him. No one…

Except…

Moose got up, and his legs took him away. They took him along the corridor and in the direction of the back door. Moose could feel the air getting warmer as soon as he neared it. He could feel his heart pulsing. He breathed in the air, his rigid muscles becoming hopeful.

He opened the door to the backyard. His eyes were closed. He could already see his tree in his mind's eye. Opening his eyes, he prepared himself for the one person who would understand him.

No…

For a split second, he didn't know what to do. Mouth open, he gazed at the tree that crept in front of him. A tree with no leaves. He stepped closer, navigating his way through the stream of rotten apples that lay on the ground. He looked around. It felt painful; his heart winced.

Around the trunk of the tree was a stream of weeds. It had grown into a thick, thirsty bush now. It covered his tree, a kind of sick cloak that had managed to creep into his tree's heart. He put his arm out, and stood there, stroking his tree.

If only. If only he had cut those weeds a long time ago. If only, he would still have his tree with him. Why hadn't he cut those weeds that day? Why did he have to feel sorry for those… *those* weeds?

Still stroking his tree, he thought about all the magical things it meant to him. To Moose, it was his guardian. Timmy's birthday. Moose's promotion. His wife's pregnancy. Wherever Moose had gone to, his tree had gone with him.

But now, even his tree had gone. Forever.

Moose brought his hand to his arm, trying to pinch himself. No. He wouldn't cry. He wouldn't…

Moose fell to the ground like a broken puppet. He put his hands to his face and cried. Everyone had left him. Nobody was there to hold him. Nobody cared about him. Nobody loved him. In that split second, he thought about all the people he had lost.

His wife.

His parents.

His Timmy.

His Sally.

His dear tree.

Tears flooding out, Moose thought about how life had changed so fast. He just wanted to go back to his old, normal life. Oh, how he wished he could live that life again? Would he be able to? Would he get that life back?

Moose looked up at the sky and tried to speak. Nothing came out, just a few sobs and an expression-filled face, but nothing else.

He wanted to ask Him if he was right. Should he really suspect Sam? Should he really suspect Sam, only to ruin his world?

Expectantly, Moose's face pointed upwards for a long time. It was like he was waiting for a reply. But, an answer didn't come.

Was He still listening?

Moose looked down. Maybe, He wasn't listening. Maybe, He had left him too. The wind began grazing at faster speeds now. It flew past the trees. It blew at Moose's face. Moose sighed.

A small piece of paper landed next to Moose's feet. Moose had a feeling he knew what it was, as soon as he realized it was smooth and shiny. He was filled with guilt. The poster that Timmy showed him. The guilt swept up as Moose leaned forward to take the piece of paper. He turned it around.

His face rose up, seeing what was written on the poster. The answer had come. He was listening. He was listening! Moose looked up at the sky, cupped his hand, and cried. Not with sadness this time, but with the happiness, the sheer happiness, of knowing he had someone in his life.

He looked at the paper once more.

COME ON, NOW. IT'S TIME TO ACT.

14

CLICK-CLACK. CLICK-CLACK. Moose's strong footsteps echoed around the house. Head held high, shoulders rising every second, Moose walked to his room. His steps were bold. His breathing was powerful. He knew what to do. He knew.

He got into his room and took out what he needed. They were small, but, at that second, he knew what he had to do with them. He set the garbage cover, scissors, and pencils out on the bed and leaned over them with pride. And then he started. Bending down, he began his work. He cut with newfound speed and vigor. He glued with an intense fury. He sketched with never-ending determination.

Moose looked at his work, his head leaning to one side, deep in thought, just like a woodpecker. No. It wasn't ready. He bent down once more and added some finishing touches.

In the end, he stood back and admired his masterpiece. It was ready. Moose's heart flooded with a sense of satisfaction.

With a quick pace, he turned back and grabbed a pair of black sports pants and a black jumper from his wardrobe. Yes. These would be perfect.

He put them all on—the jumper, the pant, and the masterpiece he had made. He took a look at the mirror.

This was it.

And he meant it. Moose was impressed by his own

creativity. Fitting snugly onto his head, his newly made mask seemed like it had come from a movie. From two holes near the center of the garbage bag, you could see his eyes. Below that, his jumper and pants finished the camouflage act. Moose shook his arms, more out of excitement than anything else.

He stared at his eyes in the mirror. Somewhere inside those blue eyes, he saw courage. He finally saw strength.

Moose stepped out of his room. Before he left the corridor, he turned his head towards Timmy's door.

He had been awful to his son, hadn't he? For some time, Moose was lost in thought.

Then, Moose's face turned to the living room. He knew how he could bring a smile. He stepped into the living room. Across the floor filled with the evening shades he walked and grabbed the pen from the floor. Timmy's pen.

The pen had been bent by the collision with the wall. Its side compartment had come off.

Side compartment?

Moose fumbled with the pen and put it close to the window's light. The side of the pen had come out. Instead of the blue color that the entire pen had, this space was silver. Metallic silver. Circuits and wires went around from one edge to the other. One of the wires was torn, and the metal jutted out dangerously. There was something written at the top. Moose squinted to see what it was.

On the side were three letters.

G.

P.

S.

GPS. Moose thought about those three letters. He stared outside the window, eyes distant, and thoughts flooding his mind. So, Sam *had* been trying to track his little Timmy. Taking a glance at the pen again, Moose thought of that voice inside him. That voice had always told him there was something wrong with Sam. But he didn't believe it. Until now.

Moose kept the pen on the table and went back the way he had come. He could still bring a smile, even without the pen. He stood in front of Timmy's door, just looking at it for some time. He brought his hand up but stopped. He knew he was Timmy's father, but something made him a little worried. Would Timmy be angry?

He knocked on the door, very slowly, with the hope that his slow pace may just be enough to remove Timmy's anger. The pieces of the torn Father's Day card were staring at him from the ground, chiding him, telling him it won't be enough.

CLICK. The bolt opened, and as quick as a bolt of lightning, something ran to him and hugged him. He looked down at Timmy. Timmy had his eyes closed. Moose closed his eyes too. He didn't want to forget that moment. Putting his arm around Timmy, he said, "It's OK, Timmy. It's OK. You'll be my little Tim Tim no matter what."

Timmy looked up at his father, smiling.

And then, he laughed. "Daddy, are you going to the comic con?"

Moose looked surprised for a moment. Why was Timmy asking… oh! He had forgotten to remove the mask he had made. He clenched it off.

"I have to go somewhere, Timmy."

"Where, Daddy?"

Moose didn't speak for a moment. He just looked out through the window. Finally, he said, "To the Haunted House, Timmy." It was like Moose had put on another mask, a mask of seriousness.

"Why?" came Timmy's next question.

Moose still did not look at Timmy. "It's time I did something I had to do a long time ago."

"Can I come with you, Daddy?" Timmy asked, eyes glistening with hope.

"No, Timmy," Moose said, smiling. "It's something I have to do alone." Moose ruffled Timmy's hair.

Timmy's last word was filled with desperation. "Daddy, I'll be a good boy. I *promise!*"

"No"—Moose started walking to the door—"you can't, Timmy." Moose felt a tug on his shirt. Timmy's eyes looked glassy, pleading to him.

"No, Timmy. No. And that's that." Moose put his mask back on and pulled the front door open.

He stepped out of the door, heart racing. Just as he was about to leave, he stopped.

Would he be coming back? Would this be the… last, the last time he walked out of his house? His breathing shallowed. He turned around and looked at his son's eyes once more.

15

Moose gripped his black backpack tightly. Looking around, he started biting his lip. Blackness. Darkness. Everywhere. His backpack made a scratching sound as it slid from right to left, following the natural rhythm of Moose's steps. It was too light to stay steady. After all, it only contained a torch, a pin, and a black eyeliner (just in case Moose needed a stealth makeover—just in case).

HOWL. Moose jumped. At that sound, he glanced around from side to side. Then, he sighted the moon in the sky. The full moon. Moose thought of what he had told Timmy, on that Halloween day not long ago. Gulping, he gripped his backpack even tighter. But, suddenly, he thought of Sam, and he quickened his pace.

In the middle of the road to the Haunted House, he turned around and looked back. Had he followed him?

Moose straightened his gaze towards the mud path. He didn't know why, but the road felt longer than usual. As the end of his energy came nearer, he saw the end of the path. And the pointed, skeleton-silver gates of the Haunted House.

With the reassurance of sight, Moose stepped into the shadows of the trees. He crouched, daring not to even breathe a little louder than usual. His black outfit made him merge with the shadows of the branches. Stepping closer, he bent down and waited behind a bush. It was going to be easy getting into the Haunted House. After all, he knew he didn't have to worry about the guard. He still remembered the last time he had seen the guard. Moose smiled. With a dog, he added. This was going to be too easy. His eyes were hammered to the front gates of the house, he looked nowhere else.

Oh… no.

He stared at the guard, mouth open. Shook. The new guard wore black from head to toe. He had black sunglasses on, even though it was nighttime. His thick build and muscles that looked like iron were covered with a black top, and below that, he wore black jeans with a tightly pulled black belt. His shoes were polished so much that they shone, even in the darkness. And on top of all that, he had decided to don a bandana.

GULP.

The guard pulled out a black, rectangular device from his (black) belt and put it in front of his mouth. He looked around, silent. Then, seeing that someone had picked up, he said, "Hello, Boss. This is Joe." He looked around before continuing. "Everything clear. Should I shut the gates?" The guard placed the walkie-talkie near his ear. A buzz from the other side. Hearing this buzz, he nodded. Putting the device back onto the belt, he stepped up to the gate.

Moose looked around, and his eyelids were pulled out as much as they could be. He bit his lip. The guard was going to close the gates! What would he do now? He shuffled in the darkness. His leg got caught in a twig. *SNAP.*

The guard's eyes turned in the direction of the bush. The guard was a cat that had heard the sound of a bird. His head movement was so fast, so swift, so agile, that Moose wondered why his neck hadn't come off in two pieces. The guard brought the torchlight's blare on the face of the bush that Moose was hiding behind. Like the reaper, he took one step forward at a time. A single step, a single second.

Moose bit his lip even harder. He turned his head from side to side, searching for an escape route. Seeing none, he put his hand to his forehead. *CRUNCH. CRUNCH. CRUNCH.* The guard was getting closer. No, no, no, no. His heart seemed like it was going to beat out of his heart. He crouched, in defeat.

And that's when he saw the lifebuoy he had been searching for. There, sitting on the ground, was his bag. And it had something that could save his life, the black eyeliner. Moose took it out of the bag at the fastest pace of his life. He opened it, took off his garbage-cover mask, and, without even thinking twice, he scribbled with it over his face. He made a sharp extension from the side of his lips. Then, he drew some cracks from his eyes. He quickly glanced over the bush. The guard was close, but he still had some time left. Just for effect, he drew some crackling lines from his mouth. Blood. Or, at least, he hoped they looked like it.

He didn't have a mirror, but he wished (or rather prayed) that he resembled a cruel, man-eating, horrifying, hateful, horrendous (OK, that was enough) joker. Moose dropped dead, coffin-style, and crossed his arms over each other in front of his chest. He closed his eyes just as he heard the bush being rattled by the guard. *CRUNCH. CRUNCH. CRUNCH.* It was those same footsteps again. Only, they were louder this time, much louder.

"Who's that?" the guard called out.

Moose didn't even dare to breathe.

"Who… Who's that?" the guard asked again, a tremble lying underneath his voice.

CRUNCH… CRUNCH… CRUNCH. Moose felt the guard's breath on his face. The guard was bending down to inspect him. Moose's hairs stood on end, like a cat's.

Three…

Moose gulped. Two…

And one. Moose opened his eyes as much as he could, hoping it looked weird and supernatural. He grew his smile as much as he could too. It pained, but Moose didn't think about that.

For a second, he had some doubts. Was the guard trying to scare him, or was the guard's eyes actually bulging out of his head? The guard's lips went up and down, twitching. Gasping, the man recoiled back.

"Hello, Joe," Moose said in a low, resonating pitch. "Remember me?" Before the guard could get any further, he grabbed his collar. The front button of his black shirt popped off and fell down, and just like that button, the guard, fainting, started falling down too. Moose switched off his evil-joker mode and tried to hold the guard upright. No. He lost his grip. The guard was too heavy. With a plop, the guard cruise-landed onto the floor.

Moose stood up, wondering. He didn't think that would work. Never. Wow, he thought. Those things they show you in films actually work.

Stepping to the front gate, and crouched, Moose pushed it open. He stepped in with the end of his feet.

HOWL.

He, and his heart, stopped. He took his foot back. Did he want to go in?

He kept his foot back in. He *was* going inside. Slowly, collecting courage from the unknown corners of his feeble body, he put both feet in.

Moose marched courageously to meet the front door. He was going to do it. He looked up at the house that loomed in front of him—the Haunted House.

The house was bathed in the spill of darkness. In the spill of darkness, except for a small window at the top which was radiating a fluorescent orange light. Moose stopped. His feet took a step back instinctively. He kept his eyes drilled on the window. It wasn't the window that scared him, it was the silhouette. There. On the left side of the window. A silhouette looking down at him. A *plump* silhouette looking down at him.

Moose shook his head. Blinking, he opened it again. He stared at the window where the orange light had been a few seconds before. Now, there was no light. No silhouette. No one.

Moose's gut twisted and turned. The windows seemed to be watching him, scanning him carefully. He stepped into the shadows of the shrubs siding the walk.

As he walked forward, his feet a tad bit heavier now, he thought about how childish he was. Everything until now was a game for him. Just a joke. But this? This was serious.

Moose closed his eyes. Did he want to keep going? Did he really want to do this?

He opened his eyes, his mind made.

"Sam, it's either me or you tonight." He broke into a run to the front door.

16

Moose stood in front of the large door that was the entrance to the house—the Haunted House. Moose shivered. He stood there, hand on his chin, thinking. The front door was easier to take, but Sam could be right in front of the door for all he knew. He wasn't going to let himself get caught by Sam so easily. Moose stared at the floorboards, trying to come up with a solution.

He knew! The backdoor! Sam wouldn't be expecting him there.

Moose: 1

Sam: 0

Moose crept and walked along the side wall. The night blinded him, and he couldn't take more than a single footstep, fearing a dug hole or something… even worse. Who knew what was out there? A kidnapper could have placed anything in front of their house.

Just as he reached five feet from the backdoor, he remembered something. He. Had. A. Torchlight.

Yep.

In his bag.

Moose sighed. Why was he so careful in the dark when he had a torchlight in his own bag? Moose put his hand into the bag and took it out. He fumbled to switch it on. In his hurry, it fell down onto the floor. *RINGGGGGG.* The noise echoed across the entire field surrounding the Haunted House. Moose froze. Had someone heard? Moose clenched his teeth, waiting for the smallest hint of movement, for Sam. In the few (quiet) seconds that followed, Moose understood that he was fine. He bent down and grabbed the torch, hawk-fast. As if he was safe if he did everything quickly.

He switched on the torch. It's hazy light now giving his eyes a rest, he got nearer to the door. He looked at the handle, wondering how he would open the door now. Ah-ha! Moose got an idea. Slowly, he took out a pin from his rucksack. He twisted it, smiling at his own ingeniousness.

Moose: 2

Sam: 0

He put the pin into the keyhole and turned it around. To the left. To the right. Yes. He was getting it. He was getting it!

No. The pin got stuck! Moose tried to wrench it out, but it didn't budge. Angrily, Moose rattled the door. *RATTLE, RATTLE, RATTLE.* Didn't budge. Not an inch. Holes of frustration stitched themselves across Moose's body. Ugh. Moose grabbed the handle, and pushed it up and down. Only, he wasn't standing the next second.

Moose landed on a wooden floor. Rubbing his cheeks as he got up, he looked behind him. Moose got a revelation; the door… was open all along. He had tried the pin, but the door wasn't locked. He felt a bit foolish (insanely foolish), but he decided that luck was with him tonight.

Moose: 3

Sam: 0

Moose picked up his torchlight from the floor and swept the darkness with its shade. A table made its place in the middle of the room. At one corner stood a sparkling sink, and next to it stood even more sparkly marble slabs. There were a few knives and blades, polished and hanging by a hook.

A kitchen.

Moose snailed his way forward. He didn't make a noise, worried that he might annoy the choking silence in the room. The silence was breaking his eardrums apart. He could hear his own heartbeat. And it was beating a lot.

He stepped into the next room… and nearly fainted. Mouth open, he gazed around. A glistening chandelier took up more than half of the room's height, which was extraordinary in its own right. Would Moose's head bend enough for him to see the top of this room? Moose looked at the two stairs that snaked their way up the middle of the hall. Portraits of men and women in white coats and stethoscopes hung around it, finely planned and placed. Moose stepped forward, feeling the soft, velvet carpet dressing the floor, engulfing the sound of his boots.

Moose's mouth was still open. He doubted if he could ever close it. Each wall in the House told a story, an ancient, historic story. Moose looked at the black clothes he wore as camouflage, expecting to see a royal robe, for that was what the room seemed to be—regal. But somewhere behind this veil of goodness was a secret. Moose could smell it. He could see it. He could breathe it. A mystery, somewhere in these walls.

Moose's eyes were magnetized to the statue in the center. A man in a Greek robe, holding a scroll in one hand, a rod with snakes in the other. Moose knew who it was. He ought to, having been the star employee of a medical company. Asclepius, the Greek God of Medicine, and his rod. But Sam had made his own changes to the statue. On Asclepius's head was an insult: a red-and-yellow pointed hat. Sashes of the same colors slithered around Asclepius' hands and legs. Moose went closer to the Greek god, suspecting another, and subtler, change. He shook his head, seeing it. Little, dark indentations spotted Asclepius' rod in a straight line from top to bottom. There were holes. It wasn't the rod of Asclepius. It was the flute, the rod of the Piper.

Moose left the derogation behind, and, sticking to the sides, he drew forward. Bit by bit, he trespassed into the old hall, a lecture room of sorts, with skeletons, organ models, and anatomical models harvested everywhere. There was so much more to ponder over, but Moose knew he wasn't here to sightsee. He was here for a reason far greater than that. As he passed by the sides, he saw many doors. But one out of them was ajar. A yellow light shone from inside. And, right after it, there were some more portraits. And then a grand staircase after all the doors.

Moose put his leg up to place his first step on the staircase.

Wait.

An open door? With a light? Moose retraced his route back.

He passed each door. The first one, no lights. The second, no lights either. Moose kept walking back. He reached the kitchen.

Wait.

Where was the door with the lights? Moose shivered. The door with the light had, Moose's thoughts stammered, dis— dis—disappeared.

Moose didn't look around anymore but instead rushed to the staircase. He didn't want to stay around here for long.

Moose took the first step up the stairs. *CREAK.* Moose winced. It was only a creak, but it felt as loud as a scream. Moose took the second step. *CREAK.* Again.

CREAK. CREAK. CREAK. Moose looked at the portraits on the wall as he made his way up. It was impossible not to, how much ever he tried. After all, the portraits were enormous, too enormous to ignore. There were grandiloquent and picturesque photos of old healers and nurses. They had pointed faces, sharp noses, and thick hair. And, without doubt, eyes that followed you everywhere. There they were, following Moose at that very instance.

CRACKLE, RACKLE. The thunder bolts had started rolling down. With a sudden flash of lightning, the whole room was illuminated, but the light abandoned Moose as soon as it had come. There it was. There it left.

CREAK, CREAK, CREEEAAAAK. The last scream was louder with the weight that Moose put pulling himself up to the first floor.

As soon as Moose got himself 'comfy' (as if that was even possible), he heard it, a buzz. *ZssSZZZZZsZSSZZZZssZZZZ.* What was that?

Moose didn't have to look far. He saw it wedged between two long sofas and a couple of indoor plants. Its face was filled with the gray anger of grains. On top of this, it cast an evil glow over the entire place, a ghost-silver glow. But this wasn't enough for it. It still kept buzzing. *ZZZZZssZZsSSSZZzzz.* Its furious buzz was the only sound that seemed more pressing than the pitter-patter of the raindrops bashing on the window. What was a TV doing here? And why was it switched on? In the dark?

Moose decided to ignore it. He glanced to his sides. Two long corridors drew a line from his far-right to his far-left. There were doors on each, too many to count.

ZZZZZZsssZZSSSSSZZZZZZ.

OK, that was enough. Moose decided he had to turn off the TV. He jabbed its main power switch. The buzz didn't go down immediately, but Moose knew it would go down any time now. Moose waited.

After five seconds, Moose was still waiting. The TV hadn't turned off! Moose jabbed the power switch much harder now. Still not switching off. Moose kept slashing at the button, but to no use. The TV refused to switch off.

That was… weird. He looked for the main power switch and switched it off. Take *that*, TV!

The TV hadn't switched off. Not even after he had turned off the main power switch. That was… even weirder. Deciding there was nothing else he could do but bear with the buzz of the TV, Moose stepped to the corridor to his left. He might not have been able to switch off the TV, but that wouldn't put him off from switching off Sam's injustice.

He went by the doors, standing in front of them with eager eyes. He would turn their knobs around one by one, but at the end of this action, he would always hear a click, a click that told him the door was locked. The clicks were numerous, and every single door that Moose passed made it. They were all locked. Moose looked at the final door on the corridor. This was it. Moose knew it, this door would open. Moose gripped the knob. He could feel it!

CLICK.

Not open. Moose sighed. He had reached the end of the corridor, and none of the doors had opened for him. The only thing left to see was a polished glass jar (filled with a thick, dirty, yellow jelly, and a round, organic something that he *didn't* want to take a guess at) and a gloomy portrait of old psychiatric wards that hung on the two opposite sides of the corridor. To the pictures' side was a locked window, the only source of light (aside from the TV) in the house. Moose glanced at the portrait, trying to see if he had a face he could share his sorrows with. Analyzing the faded colors that filled the desolate photo, colors that seemed to drip out of the frame, Moose decided he didn't and turned around. He would have to try the other corridor now.

VROOM. SWISH, SWISH. Moose stopped. What was that sound? It was coming from behind him. Taking a deep breath, he turned back before he could be scared. There was no one there. But the window, it was…

… open. Moose crouched, ready to run. But the window was bolted a moment ago, wasn't it? Or was the window open all along? Maybe, Moose hadn't noticed?

There was something weird about this house. Something…

17

Moose walked to the opposite corridor, but it took him ages. Of course, it would take ages (if you look back at the window every inch you go forward). But Moose couldn't resist the feeling. Moose tried to shiver the window-feeling away, trying to keep his thoughts to the new set of doors in front of him. He knew the procedure now: stop, turn the handle, repeat. He would do that for every door.

Before he started with the doors, he looked to his sides. Had he followed him? Yes.

Moose tried the doors, one by one. The air was filled for a long time with the sounds of the rain, the thunder, and also the sound of the clicks, those horrible clicks that came from the doors. Moose hated those clicks. Who wouldn't, when all they told you was that the door was locked?

After some time, the clicks filled Moose's brain, so much so that it felt like his mind was ringing. But he wouldn't let that ring stop him. Nor would he leave the Haunted House without doing what he had come there to do.

Moose reached the last door. Moose had no expectations by this point. The door would probably not open. Moose clasped the handle and turned it to the right. No sound came from the door.

It took a moment for Moose to…

… realize what it meant! The door was open! Moose felt like exclaiming at the top of his voice. Or doing a little jingle-dance. But he stopped himself before it was too late. You don't do a jingle dance when you are trying to catch a serial kidnapper—definitely not.

Moose stepped into the room, the bedroom. Moose knew it was a bedroom. The wrinkled bed, the lamped bedside tables, and the cozy rugs were a dead give-away. Moose tried to switch on the light.

He looked at the lightbulbs that were still dark and dolorous. Moose's shoulders slumped. OK, no lights.

Moose took a few steps forward, his eyes surveying the entire room. He looked at the back wall. A photo of Sam hung above the bed. In it, Sam had the same round glasses and stethoscope he did now, but he looked a lot younger. And he had a different sweater: a red one.

Moose then turned his eyes towards the wall on his right. Here, too, hung a portrait of Sam. It was bigger than the one above the bed (and when Moose said bigger, he was talking much bigger). It had a smiling Sam, just like the cot picture. Turning to the left, he saw the same scene: a frame with Sam in the middle. Moose didn't know what to think anymore. What do you think when you see someone who has three different portraits of themselves in their bedroom?

And it wasn't just a portrait, though. There was a newspaper cutting too. Right by the side of the bedside table. Moose went closer to have a look. The paper was musty, and it seemed a bit faded as if it was printed a long time ago. The first thing that caught Moose's eyes was the image. It was an image of Sam. But it wasn't a portrait. It was a picture of Sam standing on a stage, holding a trophy. He was smiling in this photo too. But this smile was different. 'It was…' Moose couldn't get the right word… 'more natural. More… real.'

Moose was intrigued. He read the text that accompanied the photo. As he read the article, something grew inside him. A feeling of awe. Sam wasn't just a doctor. In his previous place, he was a star. Moose understood, after reading the article, what Sam was holding in the photo. The trophy was given to the best physician-scientists in the UK. Sam was one of the best. Moose looked at smiling Sam once more. And here he was, feeling green with envy when Sam received an employee-of-the-month award, in a small, little company in the middle of nowhere. Wow, Sam was an AMAZING doc.

For a few seconds, Moose was frozen, frozen with modesty. But that was when his eyes fell on the bed. And something made them stay there. That's weird, Moose thought. A single bed. In a house with a family. Moose thought about it for some time, like some kind of detective who was about to find a clue, but he shrugged soon after. Maybe, Sam and his wife weren't doing great together. You never knew.

Moose started pulling open different drawers and cupboards. There had to be *some* evidence here of the kidnap. Somewhere. Moose flipped through multiple pages of paperwork, some notes with various medical chemistry formulas written on them, an empty personal diary, 'thank-you-doctor!' cards, a few examination reports, but nothing interesting in the least. Moose reached for the last draw.

Moose saw a paper and gripped for it. It felt rough and dusty. Moose took it out, trying to analyze it.

Five letters were emblazoned across the top of the paper, right on top of a passport-size photo of Sam. F-I-R-E-D.

FIRED.

Moose brought the paper up closer for inspection. Suddenly, a piece of newspaper that was stuck to its back slipped out and plummeted to the ground. Moose bent down to pick it.

And then, he stopped. He read it. He read the text in the newspaper, and goose bumps crept down his back. His pulse quickened. His body got intoxicated with the feeling of adrenaline.

BRITAIN'S TOP DOCTOR KILLS 20 PEOPLE.

18

Moose was holding the newspaper cutting in his hand. He wished it wasn't just a cutting of a headline. He wished that there was more text under the headline, an image, or anything else. But there was nothing—just that single headline.

BRITAIN'S TOP DOCTOR KILLS 20 PEOPLE.

Did Sam really kill people? Sam? The Sam he knew?

Moose kept the clippings back, his mind a puzzle of perplexities. For the first time that day, Moose didn't feel in control. He didn't feel like he was winning.

Moose stood in front of the bedroom mirror. He looked at his rather wavy reflection. It was probably just his eyes that made it seem wavy. After all, it was well past Moose's sleeping time. The mirror was taller than Moose and covered him from head to toe. Moose stared at his shoes and at all the dirt that had brushed against them when he had walked through the forest. Only to know that Sam was a murderer. Moose didn't think Sam could kill anyone. He might be a kidnapper, but Moose didn't think he was a murderer. That was too strong of a title.

Moose scanned the room one last time. He didn't see any evidence, any proof, or any light. There was only darkness. He had nothing else to take away. It was over.

Sam: 1

Moose: it didn't matter.

Moose looked at the door. Was he still waiting outside? He glanced at his watch. It wasn't ten minutes now after he had entered, was it?

Moose turned around, knowing he lost. He couldn't find out much about Sam. Other than the fact that he (might have) killed twenty people. He didn't think Sam did that. No…

Moose jumped.

What was that sound? What was that in the air? Moose felt goose bumps trickling over his heart. Was that a…

… scream?

Moose could hear it now. It was faint and soft, but it was there.

Moose tried to convince himself that he had not heard anything. Maybe, the screams were just his imagination. It probably was. Probably.

WAIL. Moose heard it again, and this time, his imagination went with the wind. Moose waited, stuck in time. He didn't feel like moving. Not even a single inch. All he had to do was to stay still, and everything would go away. The screams and the wails would disappear.

He heard it again—the scream. Moose turned around, fingers shaking. His heart skipped a beat. There was no one there, but Moose could hear it now. It was clear, too clear.

Moose peeked out through the window at the round disc in the sky. Seeing the full moon, he stopped breathing. Memories of last Halloween came back to him. Moose shivered. He thought of the story he had told Timmy. Why, oh, why did he tell that story that day? Now, it seemed he could… he could feel the soldier's ghosts roaming around, floating past his body with their chilly touch.

And through that chill, somehow, Moose thought of the fire that burned in his heart. He thought about why he had come here. That one thought warmed up his entire body completely. It melted the fear away. It captured him in its blaze. He knew what he had to do.

Moose took up all the courage he had, and pricked his ears up, searching for the wailing. Now that he was focused, it seemed the wailing had gotten louder. Moose stepped closer and closer to what he thought was the source of the sound. For some reason, it seemed the sound was hiding behind the walls.

But, there was only one thing that bothered him: this was the last room in the corridor. There weren't any rooms after this one. He got up to the wall. Slowly, he put his ear to it.

He could hear the scream, much, much more clearly. It was not a scream anymore. It was as loud as a shriek. He put his feet to the right, getting closer to the mirror. Moose stared at the wall. The sound was… getting louder.

Moose took another step. And another. And another. With every step he took, the sound stepped closer to him. Moose had reached the frame of the mirror now.

Moose took the final step, the step that placed him right in front of the mirror. Moose put his ear to the glass, expecting to hear nothing. But he did hear it. The wail. The screams.

Moose didn't know what to do. He rubbed his hand over the mirror frame, hoping that he would get some answers. The wails did not stop reaching his ears now. Where was the sound coming from? From another room?

Moose reached out for the glass, unconsciously, mind wandering over the problem of the source of the screams.

To his shock, his hand… his hand went right through. His hand…

… disappeared!

19

Water.

The mirror was not made of glass. As it flowed over the sides of his hand, Moose knew what the mirror was made of: water. The mirror was made of water, flowing from the top of the mirror's frame.

Moose stared through the wide gap that now formed in the mirror because of his hand blocking the water's flow. The gap stretched from where his hand was, all the way to the bottom of the mirror. It was quite dark on the other side of the hole, so he had to squint to see inside. He could just make out some steps on the floor.

Moose took his engulfed hand out. The mirror veiled its hole again, covering its secrets with it. Staring at the mirror, he finally understood why it looked wavy. It was, literally, made of waves.

And he also knew something else.

He thought about Sam and the last time Moose had seen him. He thought about what Sam was wearing. 'Oh.'

Feeling stupid and careless, Moose put his head in his hand.

How could he have thought that wearing a raincoat inside one's house was a normal thing to do? Who would wear a raincoat inside their house, or actually believe the weatherman? Moose didn't understand how he could have been that foolish…

But that was not important now. He had made that mistake, and he was not going to let Sam escape this time. He stepped back from the mirror and took a deep breath.

Sam was hiding something, and he had to know what it was.

And Moose set off. He ran to the mirror and bolted in. For a split second, he could feel the cold caress of the water on his hair, but that feeling went away within an instant.

And then, he was inside—inside what seemed to be a gigantic staircase spiraling down. At intervals, like spots on a serpent, torches jutted themselves out from the wall, casting enough orange light for you to make out the steps on the ground ('And the spirits in the air,' Moose thought!). Moose peeked over the rail-less edge of the steps, but he couldn't see the floor from here.

Moose was dripping wet. But that didn't matter to Moose now. Because blood was gushing through his veins with the heat of excitement. He did it. He did it! He was finally onto something!

But what?

Moose stepped down the stairs with the grace of a cat. Each step passed by without any commotion. There was not a sound.

Moose's feet slipped. Off he went, just inches away from the drop to the floor. Luckily, he was able to stop himself. He gulped. That was close—too close.

Extra careful now, he went down. His heart increased its melancholic beats with the passage of time. He was getting closer, and his heart knew it.

SCREAM.

Moose froze. In the silence of the secret stairs, the scream seemed to be coming from right next to him. What was Sam doing to the children?

Moose went forward, thinking about all the horrible things Sam was doing to the kids. He was probably beating them with sticks right now, making them suffer and cry. Moose had seen the movies. He knew. He knew the horror.

The sound of the screams was still there, an echo, but it was growing faint. And then, after some time, it faded away. It had gone completely. The steps were just a few with the eye, but a lot for the heart. It was an era before Moose could finally see the bottom of the staircase. And a door. Moose had not slowed down before, but he did now. For a second, he had a realization of what he was going to do. He was going to meet (and beat) a kidnapper for real. This wasn't a movie, this was real.

He took a deep breath. Shaking his hands, he prepared himself. It was time. Time to do this. It's time to act.

He tiptoed to the door, his mind being shattered with questions. But he was ready for whatever stood for him behind it. The door was open. Just a bit. A narrow slit of light shot out from the gap. Moose reached the door. He opened it a bit more.

CREAKKKKK.

Moose was petrified (quite literally). He didn't know what to do. The creak had been thunder that reverberated across the staircase. What if Sam had heard?

His body was stone-hard for a long time. But there was no Sam. No one came for him. No one had heard.

Moose unfroze himself. He put his eye to the gap in the door, looking in.

Moose kept staring inside. His hands, now turning dead-white, gripped the door handle as tightly as they could. He gulped. No. It couldn't be.

No! He shook his head.

No...

20

No. He wouldn't take his eyes off the gap in the door.

How could this… how could this be?

He pushed the door open and crept inside. The door creaked again, but Moose did not mind it this time. He knew it was a creak, a bad omen. But he didn't mind. He had to save the children.

There was no one in the room. (Moose would have exhaled with happiness if his lungs would let him. It wouldn't.) A white shine bleached the entire place, highlighting the various, metallic objects situated around. At the center, there was a lab table, with all sorts of vials and bottles. It was almost a rainbow of colors. No. That would not be a good description. More like *fluorescent poison,* Moose stinged. But that wasn't the only thing making Moose worried. Ten or so syringes were placed on the table, their polished needles glinting. Moose didn't like the look of them.

And he definitely did not like the thing in the middle of the room.

A surgical table.

A surgical table with a bloodstain at the side. The stain was fresh, so fresh it was still trickling slowly down the edge. *GLUCK. GLUCK. GLUCK.* It was dripping onto the floor, drop by drop by drop. Moose didn't think he could gulp anymore. He didn't have enough water in his throat for that.

Moose went near the vials and took one of them in his hand. He turned it around, wondering what world of maliciousness it had come from. There was an orange neon skull on one side of the flask, with *DANGER* written underneath it. The skull's empty sockets drilled into his eyes. It was warning him. Warning him…

SCREAM.

Moose jumped, spine trembling. The bottle fell out of his hand and onto the floor, splintering into a thousand pieces and spilling its toxins out.

Moose peeked to the right, to what he thought was the source of the sounds. At the right were ten, no… fifteen cages, all lined up frighteningly neatly against the wall.

But… why? Why were there cages here?

Eyebrows raised and eyes focused, Moose stepped closer to the first cage. Moose could see… something, yes… something inside the cage. He bent down, knees feeling weak.

SCREAM. Moose winced, but he didn't jump this time. Because he had seen exactly what was making the noise. No. It wasn't a 'what.' It was a 'who.'

In the cage ran around a young girl in a pink dress. She had a shriveled face and rough hair that looked like it hadn't been washed for days. Her tongue was put out, and she was crouching. Her arms were bent and at her sides. If Moose had bad eyesight, it wouldn't be too wrong of him to think she was a monkey and not a child. As soon as she saw Moose, her eyes widened. She leaped to the end of the cage nearest to him.

Grabbing the cage bars, she shook it violently, spitting at Moose. Moose took a step back, more in surprise than disgust.

What did Sam do to these children?

Moose left the first cage, ears red now, mind being pulled to the second one. The girl's screams increased in volume as Moose stepped away.

Moose bent down and peeked through the second set of cage bars.

He was doubtful: was the first cage really that bad?

This time, the child inside wasn't acting like a monkey. No screams. No wails. No running around. But, for all this silence, hung around something else. Something else all over his body: hair. Thick, brown hair. It was everywhere. On his hands, legs, and face.

Moose was worried now. He sprinted to the third cage.

The third cage was… weirder. It seemed to be empty. Moose bent his knees and peeked in.

There, in the middle of the cage, was a boy. He had his head on his arms. One of the boy's arms was normal, but the other was big and bulging. Several veins ripped through the bigger one, pulsating as he breathed in and out, rising and falling ever so slightly.

As Moose came closer, the boy lifted his face up. Little droplets blemished his face, and his nose was red. But as soon as he saw Moose, his eyes became orbs, widening.

Moose stepped back, gasping. No. He would know that face anywhere. No. He didn't want to admit it. No.

It was… It was… Moose couldn't make himself accept it…

It was…

… Jack.

Jack came closer to Moose. Tears fled from his desperate face.

"Uncle Moose…" Jack managed to say. Then, he looked down all of a sudden, and broke down, shattering. "Please get me out of here. Please! Please…"

All Moose could think about at that second was Jack in the orphanage—his handsome face, his smart hair, his cheery look. And here Jack was, fragile and destroyed. Like a broken piece of glass.

"Don't worry, Jack. I will," Moose said, "I will…"

Moose stood up, gripping the table next to him. He tried to steady himself. He closed his eyes. Moose felt like fainting.

But he knew he couldn't. These kids needed him. Sam's face came into his mind, and Moose grit his teeth as hard as he could. Sam was going to pay.

Moose looked down at the cage with sharp eyes, mind set on rescuing the children. The cage wasn't the typical one you see that has a creaking door. It did not have any keyhole at all. Hmm. Moose was captured in his thoughts. Was this an electric cage? It seemed to be.

If it was an electric cage, where was the button to open it? Moose looked around. Button, button, button. Where was its button?

He saw it. On the other side of the room was a tall computer with many small, red blips underneath it. Moose hoped those were buttons as he crossed the room to the small screen. Moose looked at the red blips grow in size, until, at an arm's reach, they revealed their true identities. They were indeed buttons.

But, really complicated buttons. Moose's eyes couldn't focus on one, and it kept clambering here and there. Moose scratched his head. How would he find the right button?

Moose swatted his right shoulder, face frowning with the disturbance. These flies were a nuisance. He kept his gaze on the buttons, ignoring the beasts that dared to bother him.

Should he press the one in the middle? Should he try all of them? He swatted his shoulder again, fuming. Why did these insects want to keep disturbing him? He turned around in anger.

BASH.

Moose opened his mouth to scream, but he couldn't hear it. He gripped his ear to stop the earthquake inside him. Fumbling, he patted his head. Water trickled over his hand. No. Not water. Blood. He looked at it, eyes zoning out.

He stumbled around and landed in a heap on the floor. Through the ever-growing black frame in his eyes, he looked at the person who had hit him.

It was Sam.

Sam dropped the baseball bat he was holding onto the floor. It clattered right beside Moose's chest. Then, Sam, his white coat crimson-cruel with Moose's blood, came near him, crouching down. "Hello, Moose," Sam chirped. "How's my favorite colleague, huh?" He gave Moose a very wide grin, and held Moose's cheeks, rubbing them.

And then, the smile faded. Darkness clouded Sam's eyes. He lifted his hand up as quickly as a serpent.

SLAP.

Moose fainted. The ringing was the only thing in his world.

21

Moose woke up with a start, thrusting forward.

Except… he couldn't thrust forward. Moose was frozen. He looked at his hands at his side, locked and bolted to the flat surface behind him. His eyes shot even lower, trying to understand his new surroundings.

They stopped at a dark red mark on the table.

And Moose knew. He knew where he was. He was anchored to the surgical table, to Sam's surgical table. Uh! Moose's anger engulfed him, and he threw his chest back and forth. He had to get out! Writhing, he tried pulling his hands out of their locks.

"So, you've finally woken up, Moose. I was waiting," came a voice near Moose. Moose looked at the voice—Sam, pouring bright liquids from one beaker to another. Moose pursed his lips. He looked down at the locks once more. He tried pushing his ankle against the lock. He tried twisting his arm. Come on. Break. Break, won't you?

Agh! Moose puffed, and his chest heaved low.

"You ain't getting outta there, Moose," Sam said. Whistling, he glanced at his beaker, and then kept muttering. "Now, if I pour 20 ml… no… 70 ml here… yes, should be good… yes, it should work."

Moose's eyes were trying to drill their way into Sam.

"Why, Sam?" Moose demanded. "Why are you kidnapping these children? WHY. ARE. YOU. DOING. THIS?"

Sam gave Moose a glance over the top of his glasses. Then, he threw back his head and laughed. His laughter echoed across the steel room, making Moose clench his fists even more.

When his laughter ended and his eyes returned to Moose, Sam's smile faded again. "You don't already know, huh, Moose? Really?"

Sam pointed his eyes at the vials in his hand, but his words were still pointed at Moose. "I saw you check my drawers."

Now, Sam's eyes moved their way up to Moose's.

"What?" Sam asked. "Didn't you expect there would be cameras in the room to my"—Sam looked around him, rubbing his arms—"*secret* lair?" And then, again, Sam broke into laughter. "Well, I really wish I could have also seen your shocked face when the TV didn't switch off. Or when the window opened! You must have been dead scared, heh?" Sam wiped a tear from his eye, laughing uncontrollably now. "It's a pity. I automated my entire mansion, but I didn't think of putting cameras everywhere!"

Moose just stared at Sam. Moose was searching his mind for a hold because his mind was spinning now. It all made so much sense. Moose thought about how scared he had been. So, it was all just a—

"You know, Moosey. I actually thought you wouldn't find my lab. I thought I would have to come and escort you. But what's the fun in that?" Sam cackled.

All of a sudden, he placed his vials on the table, sprang onto a revolving chair, and spun his way to Moose. "Well, Moosey. I better tell you my story. After all," Sam said, applying pink lipstick with the help of a mirror, "we are going to be here for a *long* time."

Sam put his lipstick down. Then, he got up and held Moose's chin. "And I like to build a positive relationship with my *subjects*."

Moose didn't like the way Sam said 'long'. Or 'subjects'.

Sam looked hard at Moose. "You don't know me, Moose." Sam clenched his lips tight. "You only know Sam, the quiet man who moved to Lollipop Avenue. You only know Sam, the employee-of-the-month of a small, dilapidated pharmaceutical company in the suburbs. You only know Sam, the loser." *BANG.* Sam hit the table, sending a jolt through it.

"Little Moosey, you haven't seen the Sam that worked in the most famous medico-pharmaceutical company in the world. No, you haven't. You haven't seen the Sam that was the most prestigious medic of the country." Sam twiddled his thumbs, pushing his nails in hard. Suddenly, he started combing the scarce hair at the side of his head, but his story didn't end.

"My friends and families were always awed by my work. After all, they should have been. I was working on a medicine that could, I knew it, save the world." Sam smiled, putting down his comb on his lap, and looking away at the far wall. But, as quick as a sun at dusk, his smile crept lower and lower, until it had vanished completely.

Sam returned to combing his hair, eyes forlorn. He was looking down now, down into his own life. "I had tested the medicine on all the animals I could find. And I was sure…

pretty sure… that I was as ready as I could be. I showed my work to all my peers. They patted me on the back. I had shown my work to my wife. She said I would even win the medical Nobel prize after two weeks."

At last, Sam looked at Moose.

"You know where I was after two weeks, Moose? I was…

… in jail."

A single tear dripped down Sam's parched cheeks.

22

"The medicine that I thought would change the world," Sam started, staring straight at Moose, "had just killed 20 people."

Sam repeated it once more, face in pain. "Twenty… people." His gaze was lost in the white walls of his dungeon.

"It was hard, Moose. Those times"—Sam glanced at Moose—"they were tough. My boss came to visit me once. Promised me my job, my love, once I finished my jail term. A boss and a job that… never came again. I didn't see my wife after going to jail either." Sam's face looked so hurt by the word 'jail' that Moose thought his heart had broken. Maybe… it did.

The Sam that, till now, looked at Moose, suddenly looked away, eyes low. "And… I didn't really see my… my… my son after that, too." Sam's face was all wet now, tears and sweat lashing out in a torrent of misery. Sam tried wiping everything away, but his hands were trembling themselves. "Whenever I see you with Timmy, Moose, playing, laughing, smiling… I think of why I didn't get that luck."

Memories played themselves across Sam's eyes, memories he so longed to forget. He wasn't staring at the wall, Moose knew Sam was staring at his nightmares.

"What did I do wrong? I had tested it. Tested it on all the animals I could find. There wasn't an animal I didn't test it on. What more could I have done? What more?"

For a long time, there came no sound from the man. It was only Moose's hurried breaths and the *whirr* of the AC.

All of a sudden, Sam jolted up. "But forget all that now," he said, his voice quick to blind his horrors away. "Now, I have all these subjects"—Sam swang his arms out, sweeping the room—"to test it on! I won't make a mistake again." Like a toy that had been wound up to full speed, Sam began pouring the bright liquids from flask to flask again, eyes more focused this time.

Not hearing a sound from Moose after all this elaborate story-telling, Sam shot a look at him through the top of his round-rimmed glasses. Moose couldn't hold it down any longer. He couldn't, not when Sam looked so calm.

"But, don't you ever feel like you are doing something… something terribly wrong, Sam? How could you play with the *future* of all these children?" Somewhere in his tone was a hope, a deep plead that he so dreadfully wished Sam would understand.

Sam didn't. Instead, his eyebrows were raised quizzically and animatedly. He looked like he would gag. "Funny you should ask that!" He giggled. "What do you mean by 'future,' Moosey? These kids don't have any!" Sam burst out laughing. Cackling. "Ah! 'Future.' Moosey thinks they have a future." Sam went back to scribbling in the notebook on his table, chuckling.

He dipped his eyes to Moose after a few seconds, thinking he would be laughing too. Seeing only Moose's melancholic look of hopelessness, Sam puffed. "Moose, you look very sad.

Too sad." Sam started scratching his chin, the other hand stroking his bald top.

Sam's eyes widened. "Yes! I know!" Sam shuffled forward to Moose, leaning, breathing on him now. "You need little Timothy here as well, don't you?"

Moose started, "No, Sa—"

"—I know," Sam's eyes were sparkling now. "I, the Piper of Lollipop Avenue, shall go and lure him!"

Surprisingly, Moose's were also sparkling, for he had seen it. The shadow.

Sam was turned away from Moose. "And then, and then… we can be one, big, happy family!" Sam rubbed his hands together. Moose knew he was grinning, even though he couldn't see his face. Sam stopped speaking and turned his head to the side with a half-glance, waiting for Moose to speak.

Moose didn't.

Sam turned around completely. He stuttered to Moose. "Come on, Moose! Please tell me something! Anything." Sam was inching his hands to shake Moose by the collar. He somehow restricted himself.

Moose was counting in his head. 'Three… Two… One…'

Moose looked behind Sam. He braved the loudest voice he could. "TIMOTHY!"

23

Sam was bouncing around, laughing like a firecracker. "Well, you're a jokester yourself, Moose! Nice one!"

Sam stepped up to the table, holding and twisting Moose's cheeks. "Guess who's trying to be funny? Little Moosey!" Sam grinned and turned around.

SPLASH.

"AGH!" Sam screamed, scrambling.

As Sam rocked around, Moose saw his son, vial in hand. *His* son. His Timmy! His heart swelled, pride gushing through it. Moose couldn't help but smile. He had been right to bring Timmy along.

Moose thought of how many times he had to keep looking back to see if Timmy was following him. He always was. And he knew his son would come to save him, even if he had told him to wait outside Sam's room.

His own son was rescuing him.

"Dad," Timmy started, smiling just as wide as Moose, "I called the police, just like you had wanted me to."

"That's my boy!" Moose felt tears sting at his eyes, but he kept them from spilling. "That's my boy…"

"Now, go and press those buttons, Timmy. There. By the computer," Moose added. Sam rubbed his eyes, finally managing to steady himself. Sam opened his eyes. "Quick, Timmy! Go!"

Before Moose finished, Timmy had run. He hurried to the computers. But, he wasn't running alone. Right behind him ran Sam.

Eyes filled with fear, Timmy pressed all the buttons he could see. He looked back. Sam would catch him. He knew that. He banged another button, just as Sam caught hold of his shirt.

GRIND.

Moose was overjoyed. He was freed. He looked down at his hands.

He was… not freed. The locks on his hands still grinned.

Hearing loud noises, Moose looked up. A tornado of children. They were rushing to the exit, exasperated, gasping for freedom. Moose might not have been freed. But all twelve of the children were.

SCREAM. It wasn't the children. It was Sam. Sam dragged Timmy to the floor, slamming him inside a cage. The veins on Sam's head were pulsing. His fists were clenched. He threw the cage near Moose.

Moose's heart felt weak. The father inside him was shaking. He glanced at his son's cage with fear, but Timmy gave him a frail thumbs-up from the inside.

The sounds of a siren whistled through the air now, catching Moose's attention back to the maniac in front of him. Sam was putting on his coat and his hat. No! Moose couldn't let him leave like that! Moose tried to break free once more, his teeth gritting with the effort.

Sam packed up his test tubes and papers, books, and files into a steel suitcase. For the first time, his hands seemed to be fumbling. At last, he flung the bag over his shoulder, ready, and gave Moose the eye.

"You may have stopped me from testing on all those children, Moose," Sam said, suddenly grinning, "but you can't stop me from getting more children. Just wait and see, Moose. Just wait and see." He raised his hands in farewell, giving Moose a mock salute.

BHAM.

The suitcase dropped to the floor, sliding across the tiles. Sam plummeted with it, drowning the floor in the blood gushing from the side of his head.

Moose didn't know what happened. His mind was blank.

He looked at the silhouette standing hunched over Sam's helpless frame. It held a baseball bat with both hands, now red from the impact with Sam's head. Up and down. Up and down. Its veins were throbbing. Oddly, its arms looked weird. One arm was… more *muscular* than the other. Up and down. Up and down. Its veins were throbbing.

Moose would know who it was, anywhere. It was… Jack.

Jack dropped the bat onto the floor and ran to the computer. *CLICK.* The locks on Moose's wrists and ankles came apart, at last, releasing him from his capture. And, bringing a lot of pain back. Jack rushed back, helping Moose and Timmy stand upright.

AH! Now that Moose was standing up, he realized how badly hurt he was. He held his head.

Everything was a blur. They scrambled out, climbing up the stairs, going through the hall, and rushing through the front door. The lights of the police cars parked outside dazed Moose. All he could feel was the strong grasp of hands on his shoulders, hands he didn't even know for sure were those of the police. He couldn't care.

The pain was searing, as Moose leaned against a car hood. He could just make out the police running into the house.

And everything went black.

24

Moose pulled at it, trying to get it to fit perfectly. There, he thought.

He had finally gotten his tie right.

Looking at himself in his bedroom mirror, dressed smartly, with his usual red cross and other health badges proudly perched high on his lanyard, Moose couldn't but think about how derailed he would have looked last week. He could still remember it all. The police lights. The medical vials. The dim glow of the lab. He patted his hair, bad images of his time at the hospital coming back.

Well, at least, he knew the one thing that mattered. Sally had made him know. The police had taken the *maniac* away. Sam.

Moose came to a halt.

No. He didn't want to think about it. Just thinking about it made his heart ache. With a weighted heart, he went back to adjusting his tie.

His tie. How long had it been since he last put it on? It seemed his tie was happy ever since the Boss had called him again. Glancing at the offer letter on the table, Moose smiled. He picked up his laptop bag, getting ready to leave for...

work. For work. He hadn't said that in a long time. It felt good to be back.

Just as he was about to walk out to the garage, he remembered! He turned around, put the laptop bag on the sofa, and hurried to the backyard. He grabbed the watering can as he rushed outdoors.

He had forgotten to water his dear tree!

As odd as it was kneeling on the ground in his suit, he didn't mind. Not when his tree was flourishing.

Moose put down the watering can, and looked up, out over the small gaps in between his tree's green leaves to the sunny sky. He smiled even wider, forgetting the shudders he felt just a week ago, standing in front of the same tree, only rotten and yellow.

Moose patted his tree's trunk, and gently placed his hand over his imprint on the bark.

Huddling close to his fingers were two other hand marks. One was his Timmy's.

And the other, still looked fresh. It wasn't long now after it had been cut out.

As the voices of children chirped through the air, Moose looked up. Timmy and Jack were rushing to him, waving two cards in the air.

"Happy Father's Day!" they screamed, putting each other's hand-drawn card over the other, vying to show Moose their love's efforts. Moose's smile couldn't become any bigger. He got Jack and Timmy near him and started ruffling their hair. Moose didn't know why, but it felt the air had gotten warmer, filling him with hope, like a fireplace in winter.

He was a father of two now, Moose rejoiced. Jack was always Moose's son, but Moose had never thought of adopting him.

Silently, Moose looked back at the newest imprint on the tree, glad he had finally done it.

Timmy and Jack pecked Moose on the cheek. He had to close his eyes, for he was in love with that second. At that moment, it seemed like all the good things in life were coming together. That second was greater than any amount of money Moose could get. That second was more precious than anything else! How much would he have given to get those kisses?

Moose said a sad 'bye' to Timmy and Jack. He didn't want to leave them to go to work, but he was also singing to go back to the office. Walking out through the front lawn, Moose waved chirpily to Sally, who was standing by the front yard. Sally gave a huge smile, but Moose could still spot how red her cheeks were; she was embarrassed. He had told her not to be, but she still was.

REV, REV. Moose put his feet down on the throttle and reversed the car out of the lot.

He passed the tree on the front of Lollipop Avenue, but, instead of taking the turn he always took to work, he crossed off to the other side of the road. Moose knew where he was going. His first stop was not the office.

Houses and lanes, lawns and fields, fells and cows. He passed all of them, not pressing the brakes even once. He kept driving, leaving his side mirrors a blur of the countryside. He knew where he was going.

He pressed on through the cobblestone roads, through the empty streets, and the quiet buildings. And then, finally, he stopped his car. Getting out, he looked at the top of the building he longed for.

Moose knew where he was going. He was going… home.

Moose took a look up at the great, grand church spire in the distance, glinting in the bright sunlight. Home.

His body and heart feeling as light as air, he entered its grand chamber. Kneeling on the marble floor, he kept his eyes transfixed on the altar. Quietly, magnified by the room's power, he looked on.

Moose closed his eyes, thinking about all the magical things in his life that he was grateful for. All the good things. All the happy moments. All the smiles, all the joys. All the people who loved him, all the people he loved. All the luck he had, and all the good he could do. He shut his eyes more tightly, partly with the fear that his feelings would vanish if he opened them, partly not to cry.

He hadn't forgotten those words. He didn't think he ever could.

COME ON, NOW. IT'S TIME TO ACT.

How lucky was he? Would he ever want to be anyone else, Moose thought, certain of the answer.

Moose opened his eyes, the chirp of birds awakening him, and let the colorful sunshine of the stained-glass windows embrace him.

Life is good, indeed.

Epilog

HOWL. A wolf called out. The trees whistled their solemn song as they waited for anyone, anyone at all, to pass by their morbid frames. Their hands lacked any leaves, and they stood like bare sentinels, guarding the town. A bright full moon shone in the sky, bone white, casting a pale light onto the pavement. The air felt thick, heavy, and laden. Oh, what was this night?

There was only one contender to the brightness of the moon. It stood, lonely, glinting in the darkness, absorbing the blackness. Its sharp prongs were a warning. Its locked chains were an omen. Its yellowed plaque was a nightmare.

HANDSOME MANOR, it read.

In front of the gates stood a daredevil, a daredevil van. Its front lights looked on at the silver gates with menace and malice. Some of the brown, cardboard boxes on its back were open at the top, dark and endless, like Pandora's boxes of evil. A perfect van, for a perfect house.

A bald-headed man stood near the crates, hands on hips, watching as movers picked up each box and kept it near the front gates. His face was invisible to the creatures behind the bushes, but they knew they had to be careful. Slowly, the first monster got out of the hedge, careful not to rustle its leaves.

Its pristine, shining, white robe slid over the small branches of the bush. There was something peculiar about the cloth's shine. It was too bright, too white, and too… ghost-like.

The ghost looked back at the bushes and called out to… someone. Or a few 'someones.' Or… a few 'some monsters.' The bushes rustled violently, and a bandaged hand rose out, followed by a bandaged head, and a bandaged leg. Only the mummy's eyes, green in the night, could be seen on its plastered face. The mummy turned around and helped his friend out of the leaves, strongly. His friend was hairy and muscular, with a knife-gray tail, ripped jeans, and bloodshot eyes. As the mummy held his friend's hand, pulling him out over the last thorns, one could see the sharp fangs at the pincer-like ends of his hands.

The two smaller monsters joined the phantom, and the three swayed over to the bald man near the van. The werewolf smacked his lips. The mummy grinned. The phantom rubbed his hands together. It was time, time for the final delight.

As the ghost stepped towards the man, the light from a nearby streetlight fell onto the man's clothes, reflecting emphatically from his sweater. Green, the phantom thought, just like… Sam's. The ghost swept to a still, eyes distant with haunting memories.

And then, it shuddered. It didn't even want to think about it. No. Shaking its head violently, as if to shake out the feelings, it regained its momentum, glazing over to the man, glazing over for the ultimate horror.

It, and its monster cronies, were a breath away from the man. The ghost raised its white hand. It hovered its fingers over the man's shoulder, deciding where to strike. And then, it brought its hand down on the man's right arm, gripping his flesh with insane strength.

The man jolted around.

"TRICK OR TREAT!" the monsters shouted together, laughing. The ghost removed his white dress, revealing the well-kept hair and face. It was Moose. Now, with the light of the lamps removing the masks of the monsters, one could see the human qualities of their faces. The werewolf grinned, exposing its sparkling white teeth. (Evidently, this was Jack.) Timmy the mummy tore out its facial bandages.

Sighing, the man wiped his forehead. He gave out a laugh, short and sudden as if to say he was happy that he wasn't being devoured by a real monster's teeth.

"Oh, OK. I got scared for a second!" the man said. He put his round-rimmed glasses back onto the top of his plump nose and adjusted his green sweater. He wiped his bald forehead with a tissue. "I am so sorry, kids. I don't think I have any sweets with me," he said, looking at the boxes surrounding him, "I really forgot it was Halloween."

Moose flicked his hand. "No, no, no. That's alright!"

"Well, I just moved in you see," the man continued, looking back at the crates in the van. "Um, got a lot of packing to do." The man laughed, and Moose joined him. "So, what's your name?" he asked Moose.

"Mr. Phantom?" Another round of laughter.

Moose told the man his name. The man stroked his chin, looking up. "You know. I've heard that name before. Someone told me." He thought for a bit longer. "I think we're colleagues." He smiled at Moose, already ready to start working with him.

Moose looked unmoved, but, on the inside, his mind was rushing. His colleague? He inquired about where the man worked.

"Me?" the man asked, a bit surprised that Moose hadn't heard of him already. "I am joining in as the senior physician-scientist."

Moose thought, thought about what the man had just said. Senior physician-scientist… Sam's role. The title swarmed around in Moose's mind. 'Senior. Physician. Scientist. Senior. Physician. Scientist.'

Timmy's pulls on Moose's sleeve hurried the thoughts away.

"OK, then. I better leave," Moose said, the pulling from Timmy getting more intense. "Anyway, see you at the office. I hope you love Lollipop Avenue."

Moose didn't know if it was real, or if it was his mind's joke. But, the man's eyes suddenly turned a shade darker. He joined his hands together, rubbed them slowly, and said, "I am sure I'll love it."

OK. Weird.

Moose was grimacing in his mind, but he didn't show it on his face. Silently, he tried to slip away from this… this man. He turned around, but he suddenly remembered his manners and turned back. "Sorry," Moose started, "I didn't get your name."

"Oh. I forgot," the man said, "My name is Sammy. Dr Sammy Hampton."